Nicole took a deep breath.

She was physically ready to walk into Liam's bookstore, but her emotional readiness was a different story. She wanted to project confidence and poise. Things that had never been a problem... until she married a man who was more likely to criticize than he was to compliment or encourage her dreams and desires.

She opened one of the glass French doors of Sip & Read. It was a magical bookstore with redbrick walls partially covered with old plaster that had chipped away in large chunks, a high ceiling covered with pressed tin squares, dark woodwork and an eclectic mix of antique shelves. Liam waved from behind a coffee bar that looked as if it were made from hardcover books. Last night, he'd said *we'd* lived over the bookstore, but did that include a wife? If he was still married, she'd be forced to ignore the temptation, and that would be a good thing. She couldn't be running around lusting after a man when she was so recently widowed. It would only give people a reason to talk.

But what if she told everyone the whole story? Maybe they would understand. She shook her head and walked toward Liam.

She wasn't ready to share her secrets.

Dear Reader,

Welcome back to Oak Hollow, the Texas Hill Country town where people often discover they've come home. I've had so much fun creating this fictional small town full of loving and quirky characters. *The Bookstore's Secret* is the sixth book in my Home to Oak Hollow series and can be read as a stand-alone, but if you haven't already, you can catch up with other characters in the first five books.

Nicole Evans and her nine-year-old daughter have temporarily moved back to her small hometown while waiting to see if she got a prestigious pastry chef position. When the guy she's loved from afar since she was a teenager asks her to help reopen his bookstore's café, she can't say no. Single dad Liam Mendez finds that having Nicole work for him is harder than expected. His heart wasn't supposed to get so involved with a woman who is not staying in town.

At this point in life, Nicole needs a friend more than a lover, but after an unexpected night in the same hotel room, the bookstore's kitchen isn't the only place where things are heating up. While working in his office, she discovers Liam wrote last year's bestselling romance novel under a supersecret pen name. He hates attention, and she promises not to tell anyone... but accidentally reveals his secret. And the press arrives. How will Nicole and Liam get back on the same page and start a new chapter together?

Thank you so much for reading!

Best wishes,

Makenna Lee

PS: I love hearing from my readers. You can find all my social media links on my website, makennalee.com.

The Bookstore's Secret

MAKENNA LEE

Recycling programs
for this product may
not exist in your area.

ISBN-13: 978-1-335-72440-3

The Bookstore's Secret

Harlequin Enterprises ULC
22 Adelaide St. West, 41st Floor
Toronto, Ontario M5H 4E3, Canada
www.Harlequin.com

Printed in U.S.A.

Makenna Lee is an award-winning romance author living in the Texas Hill Country with her real-life hero and their two children, one of whom has Down syndrome and inspired her first Harlequin book, *A Sheriff's Star*. She writes heartwarming contemporary romance that celebrates real-life challenges and the power of love and acceptance. She has been known to make people laugh and cry in the same book. Makenna is often drinking coffee with a cat on her lap while writing, reading or plotting a new story. Her wish is to write stories that touch your heart, making you feel, think and dream.

Books by Makenna Lee

Harlequin Special Edition

Home to Oak Hollow

A Sheriff's Star
In the Key of Family
A Child's Christmas Wish
A Marriage of Benefits
Lessons in Fatherhood

Visit the Author Profile page
at Harlequin.com for more titles.

To Jackie and Lee,
the best in-laws a girl could ask for.

Chapter One

Grieving a husband that you're upset with was a multifaceted emotion, much like the many faces of a sharp-edged crystal, but Nicole Evans was finally in the driver's seat of her own life with plans to steer it in a new direction.

After one humiliating but necessary detour.

Nicole—once a PTA mom, homeowner and pastry chef—winced at the twinge in her back as she heaved the overpacked suitcase onto one of the twin beds in her childhood room. Driving for two days had taken a toll on her body and mind. Each mile from Montana had layered on a little more weariness and fear of being the latest topic of whispers and sideways glances in her small Texas hometown.

The same cherrywood furniture filled the room. Two twin beds with a nightstand between them, two dressers and a desk. But rather than lavender, the walls were pale blue with crisp white trim around the deep-sealed windows. The curtains and bedding where soft shades of blue and gray, making the room soothing. Something she could use a whole lot of right now. On the wall where her hard-earned ribbons and certificates had once been, now hung a large landscape painting signed by local artist Alexandra Walker.

It was January 2, and barely a week ago they'd been here for Christmas. All the decorations still adorned the house inside and out. It had been a wonderful holiday with her family, but the day after flying home to Montana, the final stroke of bad luck had her packing what she could in her SUV and driving back to Texas.

The wooden floor in the hallway creaked with approaching footsteps. "Mommy, am I sleeping in here with you?"

Nicole opened her arms to her nine—going on twenty-year-old—daughter, Katie. Her long chestnut hair was tangled from too many hours in the car. "You certainly can if you want to, or Jenny's old room can be yours." Nicole glanced at the second bed tucked under the windows and remembered how her niece, Jenny, would sleep there when she was scared.

With her thin arms still around her mother's waist, Katie looked up and twisted her mouth into a thoughtful expression. "I think I should stay in here with you. At least for the first night."

"Good plan, Katie Cat." She hugged her close once more before letting go.

"Mimi said supper is ready."

Nicole knew she should eat, and her mom's stew was delicious, but exhaustion was rapidly claiming her. She longed for a hot bath, and then all she wanted to do was crawl into bed and sleep for days, especially now that she had someone who could look after her child while she rested. Truly rested. Not the one-eye-cracked sleep she'd been subsisting on for weeks. She glanced from her suitcase to the door.

She'd come this far, and a few more minutes of consciousness wouldn't kill her. Hopefully.

"Come on, Mommy." Katie tugged her hand. "You have to eat. Mimi said you're too thin."

"She said that?" Nicole glanced down at her own body. Her jeans were hanging a little low on her hips, and she couldn't afford new ones. "Okay. Let's go eat."

In the hallway, she paused momentarily in front of her wedding photo hanging on the wall in a silver frame. She'd been so happy and in love. Her heart ached for the old times before Jeff's true nature had come out and he'd become controlling and basically turned into someone she no longer knew. Their marriage had become a facade. She'd lost that man in the photo long before his death. But because she'd been too embarrassed to say anything, no one knew the truth of her turbulent marriage.

As they came down the stairs, the savory scent of home cooking made her mouth water.

Maybe I'm hungrier than I thought.

Her mom, Mary Winslet—who most people called Mimi—was moving around the eat-in kitchen, putting corn bread and salad on the sturdy rectangular table that had been in the two-story white farmhouse for seventy years. She'd done a bit of remodeling and freshened things up over the past year. The cabinets had a new coat of white paint, and the butcher-block countertops of her childhood had been replaced with light granite that looked almost like marble. The hardwood floors were varnished to preserve the years of wear. Her mom had chosen to leave all the dents, scrapes and gouges because she said they were a road map of her life.

Nicole ran her big toe over the dent from the time she dropped a pipe wrench while helping her dad fix the kitchen sink. "The house looks really great, Mom."

"Having a grandson-in-law with a restoration and construction company is very handy." She tucked her brown hair behind her ear, now liberally streaked with silver and curlier than it had been before cancer treatments a few years ago.

"Eric does great work. When will they be home from their vacation?"

"In four days. Jenny will be so happy to have you home." Mimi poured glasses of lemonade. "Grab a bowl. They're already out of the cabinet and beside the pot of stew."

Nicole helped her daughter then filled her own bowl before taking a seat in the same spot she'd used her whole life. It had a view of the orchard out the window on her left, and across from her was the empty chair her older sister—ten years her senior—had used until they lost her years ago. When her sister died in an accident, Nicole's baby niece Jenny had come to live with them and basically been raised as her sister.

Mimi stopped behind Nicole and kissed the top of her head and then Katie's. "I'm so glad to have both of you home with me."

Home.

Nicole flinched. She loved being here with her mom, but the realization that this was now the only home she had made her throat burn.

I should be thankful. Not whining.

Having a safe place to regroup was more than some people had. "It's really good to be here. I'm lucky to have a home to come to." She took a bite, and the flavors of savory beef and vegetables blended into a lovely dance on her tongue.

Mimi sat at one end of the table. "It will always

and forever be your home, sweetheart. I still wish you had told me you'd made a decision and were driving from Montana. I could have flown out and driven with you."

"I know, Mom. But you just paid for the plane tickets for us to come home for Christmas, and you were in Montana six months ago for Jeff's funeral. Plane tickets are expensive. We did fine. Right, Katie?"

"Yep," her daughter said around a mouthful of corn bread. "We took care of each other, just like we always do."

An ache started in Nicole's chest. She loved that her daughter was a natural caretaker, but she hated that because of the relationship Katie had observed between her and Jeff, she felt the need to look after her own mother. A major part of her new life plan was to set a better example for her child.

Nicole sighed, so much weariness in one sound. "I did call and tell you when we were on our way to Texas."

"But not until you were already on the road." Her mother's pursed lips conveyed her displeasure.

"Mimi, we listened to a whole bunch of audio books," Katie said. "One of them was a mystery, and I guessed who the bad guy was."

"I love a good mystery. Tell me about it."

Nicole let them talk about stories and characters and drifted into her own thoughts. A place that could be dangerous as of late. She'd known her mom would be upset about her waiting to call, but honestly, she had needed the drive to think and prepare for whatever this unexpected return to the Texas Hill Country had in store, but the time hadn't helped much. She had not returned—as she'd claimed she would—as a successful chef. Although she had worked in kitchens of restaurants and a resort, she had not been in charge. Never been *the chef.*

Her husband had accused her of wasting money on culinary school, but he sure hadn't minded eating what she cooked. She could not under any circumstance let him be right.

Her daughter patted her shoulder. "Mommy, you're not listening."

"Sorry, Katie Cat. I'm just tired. What did I miss?"

"I want to see Lilly the same day they get home. I already have to wait *four* days for them to get back from vacation." In her excitement, Katie climbed onto her knees, and Nicole motioned for her to sit back down.

"We will have to see what time of day they get home." When Jenny married Eric, she had adopted his four-year-old daughter, and Katie adored her little cousin.

The doorbell chimed its five-note tune. "Are you expecting someone?" she asked her mom.

"Oh, yes. A delivery." Mimi left the table and

disappeared around the corner to the front door. "Hello, Liam."

Liam? No! An alarm shrieked in Nicole's head.

She considered running upstairs, but her mother had just told him she and Katie were in the kitchen and invited him in. She hastily yanked the hair band off her wrist and tried to tame her riotous curls into a ponytail, and then she swiped her fingers under her eyes in case her mascara was smudged before she remembered she wasn't wearing any makeup. Not even concealer on her dark circles.

Why did I come downstairs? I should've just gotten into a nice hot bath.

Her mom returned to the kitchen with the guy Nicole had loved from afar since she was twelve years old. For twenty-five years he'd been her fantasy man.

"Look who stopped by to deliver the books I ordered."

Katie's head shot up. "Books? I love books."

"One of them is for you," Mimi said. "But you have to finish eating first."

Liam smiled at Katie and then turned to Nicole, and her stomach fluttered with the kind of nervous sensation she'd always felt as a teenager. The years had been good to him. Very, very good. A maroon T-shirt hugged his biceps and shoulders, and her fingers tingled with the inappropriate urge to reach out and see if the denim of his faded jeans was as soft as it looked.

"Hello, Liam," Nicole said with a small wave.

"Nicole, Katie, so good to see both of you. I didn't know you were visiting."

"We're not visiting," Katie said unhelpfully. "We have to live here now."

Nicole's heart sank, and she made a mental note to once again talk to her daughter about blurting out every thought that came into her mind.

"Sit down and eat something," her mom told him. When he started to protest, she pulled out a chair and motioned for him to sit.

"I'd love some." He sat across from Nicole, in the chair that had been her older sister's, and they shared a smile as Mimi filled another bowl with beef stew.

His black hair had only the barest hint of silver above his ears, and it felt as if his dark eyes could see more than she was ready to share. Was this the start of the whispers? Not that she thought Liam was a gossip, but without warning she might have to answer the first questions about why she was back in town or discuss the disaster her life had become.

Liam accepted the bowl of stew and a glass of lemonade. "This smells delicious." He took a bite, and his face morphed into a satisfied expression that made his eyes close. "Mmm. So good."

Nicole's skin pebbled as his expression and deep,

rumbly voice made her envision him bare-chested and braced above her. It wasn't the first time she'd fantasized about Liam being that satisfied with her…in bed. She quickly ducked her head and focused on her meal.

What is the matter with me? Has being here only a few hours turned me back into a teenager?

She hadn't felt the intimate touch of a man in well over two years, long before her husband's death. It had been ages since she'd wanted anything to do with a man. Until now. As they ate, she couldn't stop sneaking glances at the way his muscles shifted with each movement. She admired his deep olive complexion against the white of his teeth when he laughed, and she liked the way he talked to her daughter about her interest—in a way that her father rarely had.

"I'm done," Katie announced. "Can I see my book now?"

"Yes. It's on the coffee table in the living room," Mimi said.

Katie put her bowl in the large apron-front sink and skipped from the kitchen.

"It's nice to see a kid so excited about books. It's certainly good for my business," Liam said, then looked straight at Nicole. His smile softened. "I'm so sorry to hear about your husband."

"I appreciate that." She couldn't hold his gaze. Every time someone expressed sympathy, a voice in her head screamed, *If you only knew the whole story.*

Mimi pushed the plate of corn bread closer to Liam. "How was your family's Christmas at your sister's new house in Dallas?"

"Very nice. With two toddlers and a new baby, there was a lot of excitement."

"Have I told you Nicole graduated from culinary school?"

"No." Ice clinked in his glass of lemonade as he set it down. "Do you have a specialty?"

"Yes. I'm a pastry chef. I was working at a resort."

"No kidding? I'm looking for a chef at the bistro in my bookstore. We offer appetizers and desserts along with wine and coffee. Are you looking for a job?"

"Actually, yes." Her stomach trembled when she met his gaze. His handsome grin widened to show dimples and fine lines at the corners of his eyes. This man knew how to make forty-one years old look really, really good.

"Want to come by Sip & Read tomorrow and we can discuss things?"

"That would be great. Is after lunch okay? I plan on taking the rare opportunity to sleep late tomorrow morning."

"I'll be there all day. We live in the apartment above the bookstore."

She was about to ask who lived with him, but

her mother stood and thankfully interrupted her intrusive question.

"If you two will excuse me, I'm going to check on Katie," Mimi said and then left them alone in the kitchen.

The air seemed to heat and crackle between them. What was this pull Liam had always had over her? And why had he never felt it too?

He took a bite and chewed thoughtfully. "I guess you'll be registering Katie for school?"

"Yes. I'll go in on Monday. I hate that she has to start at a new school in the middle of the year."

"I have a feeling she'll catch up in no time. I just registered my son a few months ago. He's not very happy about being at a high school with no swim team or photography class."

"Change can be hard for kids. Maybe he can start a photography club or something."

She'd heard that Liam was getting a divorce, but did his son going to school here mean he'd gotten back together with his wife? His left hand was wrapped around his glass, and he was not wearing a wedding ring, but that didn't mean much. She'd taken hers off months before asking Jeff for a divorce, and he hadn't even noticed.

When Nicole woke the next morning, she felt more rested than she had in months. Coming home had been the right decision. Even though it had been her only choice. Cracking her eyes open, she saw that the other twin bed was empty. She closed them again and savored a few more minutes of rest, knowing someone responsible was looking after Katie.

After a late breakfast, she took her time getting ready for her meeting with Liam. She changed her outfit three times before deciding on charcoal gray jeans and a red sweater. With her hair and makeup carefully done, she left her daughter in the pecan orchard with her mom and drove the few miles to town.

When she made it to the Oak Hollow town square, she was surprised by the lack of open parking spaces. She finally found a spot near the courthouse and made her way across the center of the square, passed the gazebo and the playground filled with happy children. Tourism appeared to be up, and they had picked a beautiful winter day to be out walking around.

The Christmas decorations would be coming down soon, but for today, the swags of greenery, lights and sparkly ornaments made the historic square look like something out of an old movie. The only thing missing was the snow she had left behind in Montana.

Being Texas, you never quite knew what weather to expect, but today was mild and she didn't need more than her sweater to stay warm. A cold breeze lifted Nicole's hair, tossing the curls she'd carefully tamed into soft waves. Leaves skittered around her feet, and the savory scent of Southern cooking drifted from the Acorn Café, the Friday lunch crowd filing in and out with happy smiles.

She continued walking along a row of businesses in historic buildings. There was a new jewelry store, an art gallery beside Jenny and Emma's dress shop and a florist with containers of chrysanthemums out on the sidewalk. Two doors down from the bookstore, she paused to look at a window display of kitchenwares. All her cooking supplies were still wedged into the back of her SUV with the other things she hadn't sold before leaving.

"Nicole."

She turned at the sound of her name.

"We're all so happy to have you back in Oak Hollow," said Mrs. Jenkins.

How did she already know I'm back?

She accepted a tight hug from the plump, elderly woman who would most definitely spread any secret or juicy bit of gossip that she heard. "It's good to see you."

"I'm so sorry for your recent loss."

"Thank you."

"I'm late for a meeting at the newspaper office. I write an advice column for them now. We'll have to find time to visit soon because I want to hear everything that's been going on with you."

I bet you do.

"Sounds good." Actually, it sounded more like she'd just set herself up for a polite interrogation, and she'd take a bet that Mrs. Jenkins's advice column included gossip.

Mrs. Jenkins hustled down the sidewalk, weaving in and out of shoppers, her long coat swishing around her calves as she moved.

Nicole waved to a cute bundled-up toddler in a stroller, wondering if the little girl's family were locals she didn't know or out of town visitors. She continued her walk along the storefronts. It's not that she disliked her hometown, because it was actually very nice, but it's not where she had planned to be at age thirty-seven. And she certainly hadn't planned to return as a widowed single mom—broke and without a home through no fault of her own. Unless you counted her poor judgment choosing to marry a man with a gambling problem. An addiction that had made a wreck of her world. She'd gotten loads of sympathy and well wishes after the logging accident… But no one knew the whole story. She hadn't even told her mom or Jenny about the day of the accident or the many months leading up to it.

She had not lost a loving husband who she missed having beside her. She'd lost a roommate who she had loved…once upon a time. But even so, she had still cried for many nights after putting her little girl to bed.

A horn honked and startled her back into the present. Nicole took a deep breath. She was physically ready to walk into Liam's bookstore, but her emotional readiness was a different story. She wanted to project confidence and poise. Things that had never been a problem...until she married a man who was more likely to criticize than he was to compliment or encourage her dreams and desires.

She opened one of the glass French doors of Sip & Read. The two-story building had originally been a hardware store in the 1920s, then a dress shop, a restaurant and then vacant before Liam bought it. It was a magical bookstore with red brick walls partially covered with old plaster that had chipped away in large chunks, a high ceiling covered with pressed tin squares, dark woodwork and an eclectic mix of antique shelves. The nutty aroma of coffee mingled with the sweetness of fresh flowers and that scent of books that can't be put into words.

Liam waved from behind a coffee bar that looked as if it were made from stacks of hardcover books but was actually bricks painted to look like the spines of famous novels. Beside it stood a glass bakery case that held a meager selection of what was probably store-bought pastries. Last night, he'd said *we* live above the bookstore, which must include his son, but did it include a wife? If he was still married, she'd be forced to ignore the temptation, and that would be a good thing. She couldn't be running around lusting after a man when she was so recently widowed. It would only give people a reason to talk. Running into Mrs. Jenkins had been a glaring reminder.

But what if she told everyone the whole story? Maybe they would understand. She shook her head and walked toward Liam.

She might never be ready to share some of her secrets.

Chapter Two

Liam Mendez sensed a subtle change in the air. Something he couldn't put a finger on. Not a sound or a scent, but more of a ripple that made his skin tingle. Turning to hand a customer his cup of coffee, he caught sight of Nicole. She waved to him but was taking her time making her way through the displays that ran down the center from the front door of the bookstore to the bistro counter.

When he'd left for college, she was just starting high school, and he'd thought of her as a kid. But now… How had he never noticed how beautiful Nicole was? He pulled at the collar of his T-shirt.

Is she the source of the shift in the air?

She'd smoothed out her curls, and her long chestnut hair was falling over her shoulders to graze her breasts. Her ivory skin glowed, and her high cheek-bones flushed a pretty pink—

Liam squeezed his eyes closed and braced his hands on the black granite countertop. Lately, he'd caught himself writing character descriptions in his head while observing people. Maybe he really should write a second book. For months, his publisher had been asking him to send something new.

"Glad you could stop by," he said when Nicole made it to the counter. "Would you like coffee? Maybe a cappuccino or latte?"

"I'd love a pumpkin spice latte." She sat on one of the four stools at the end of the counter.

"I've only recently learned to use this machine. Yesterday, I went a little over the top with the pumpkin spice syrup, so let's hope I don't make something that will turn you into a pumpkin."

That got a soft laugh from her. "Let's hope not. I look terrible in orange."

They were silent while he worked, and when he turned to give her the coffee, she was wringing her hands. He hated seeing her nervous and jumpy. Liam suspected the change in her personality had something to do with her deceased husband.

"It looks right. Let's give it a taste test. Tell me if I start changing colors." She brought the cup close and blew across the surface before taking a careful sip. "Mmm. It's very good. Next time I'll test you with a mocha latte."

"I better start practicing." He was happy his teasing had brought a smile to her face, but it wasn't the big grin he remembered. They had been neighbors and good friends growing up, but in the many years since he'd gone off to college, they had drifted apart as many childhood friends do. But he still knew her well enough to know she had changed. Once full of life and outgoing, she was now quiet and reserved. He got the feeling the change in her personality was something more than becoming a widow. Something deeper and reaching further back than a few months.

She took another sip and glanced around. "This place is amazing, and it looks like you are doing good business. You run the bookstore with your wife?"

"No. I'm divorced." There was a flash of emotion in her green eyes, but he couldn't be sure if it was good or bad. "My son, Travis, is living with me while his mother is away on a Doctors Without Borders field placement."

"I should have told you last night that I am only in Oak Hollow temporarily. I was just so tired from traveling that I wasn't thinking very clearly. So, I can't take a long-term position, because like I said, I'm only here temporarily."

She was certainly very clear about the temporary part, and for some reason that made his stomach tighten. "I probably should have told you that our kitchen is likely not what you are used to at a fancy restaurant or resort."

"I'm sure it's fine. Want to show me?"

He motioned to his newest hire, Amy, who was twenty-two and a hard worker. The ends of her shoulder-length blond hair were dyed pink, and she had a bubbly personality that the customers liked. She put one more book on a shelf and made her way over to them. "Amy, will you work the coffee bar, please."

"You got it, boss," she said with a teasing salute.

He introduced the two women and then led Nicole through to the kitchen.

Still holding her latte, she glanced around and took everything in. "It's actually bigger than I would have expected, and it's nice. There is no one working the kitchen right now?"

"No. I've had to temporarily limit the menu to things we can serve with ease. Will you take the job?"

"Yes. As long as I'm in town, I'd love to work here." She set her cup on the center work island, and he stood across from her.

"What are your plans after leaving Oak Hollow?"

"My goal is to be a pastry chef at one of the Hamilton Resort locations."

"Those are fancy resorts. I've been to one in Colorado. And I do remember the breakfast buffet having amazing pastries. Travis almost made himself sick because his eyes were way bigger than his stomach."

She chuckled. "He wouldn't be the first."

"Why Hamilton Resorts?"

"Because they are known for their food and desserts. Employees get to live in an apartment complex on the edge of the grounds, and they have childcare and afterschool programs for employees' children."

"Good perks."

"They don't have any openings at the moment but expect to have some soon. I also applied with several other large resorts."

"Nearby?"

"The closest one is in north Texas, a day's drive away from Oak Hollow."

He propped his forearms on the stainless-steel work surface, which brought him closer to her. Close enough to catch the scent of cinnamon and vanilla. Had she been baking this morning or did she just naturally smell delicious? "So… Temporary. How long do I get to have you?"

Her eyes widened and rosy patches appeared on her high cheekbones.

Way to say something suggestive, fool.

Now he had a burning urge to "have her" in a way that had nothing to do with working in this kitchen. The power of his reaction startled him. He straightened and took a few steps back.

One corner of Nicole's full lips lifted into a half grin. "I don't have a hard date scheduled."

"I'll take all you'll give me before you go." He sucked in a quick breath. "Time. All the time," he hurried to say and then turned away, not wanting her to see signs of desire on his face.

"Dad," Travis yelled from halfway down the back stairway that was flush against the back wall of the kitchen and led up to the apartment. "The microwave isn't working."

Normally, he would lecture him about yelling and interrupting, but this time he was thankful his son had put a quick stop to his untimely flirting. "I'll take a look at it, but first, come meet someone."

Travis hesitated but came all the way down the stairs, his gaze flicking between the two of them as if he expected bad news.

"This is my son, Travis. And this is my old friend Nicole. She is a chef and going to be working here." He shot her a half smile. "Temporarily."

"It's nice to meet you, Travis."

"You, too." The teenager shoved his hands in the pockets of his sweatpants. "Are you making anything for dinner?" he asked her with a hopeful expression shining in his dark brown eyes.

"He doesn't like my cooking," Liam said.

"That's because you *can't* cook," Travis mumbled.

Nicole chuckled but quickly covered her mouth.

"I probably need to take stock of the pantry and make a shopping list before I can cook much in this kitchen. But you should both come over to our house tonight." She smiled at his son. "I live in the white farmhouse next door to your grandmother."

"You live with my Abuela's friend who has the peach and pecan orchards?"

"Yes. She is my mom. I'm not sure what we are having, but I do know there will be homemade pecan pie."

"I like pie," Travis said, and brushed his dark hair back from his forehead. "Can we, Dad?"

"Sure. Travis has a sweet tooth."

The teenager scoffed. "I got it from you."

"I can't deny it." His son rolled his eyes and stomped back up the stairs, making sure to grab every opportunity to show his displeasure with having to live "out in the sticks."

"Is that him having a hard time adjusting to living here or is that just the teenage attitude I can look forward to?"

"Some of both. He wants to be back in Austin, and since his mom isn't here to see his displeasure, I get the attitude all to myself." When Nicole walked around to his side of the prep island, he had a strong urge to touch her hair.

Stop it. She just lost her husband.

He knew what could happen when someone jumped into a new relationship too soon. His rebound had been an epic failure. And as for his ex-wife, she'd started dating someone before their divorce papers were even signed. It had layered more hurt on top of her request for the divorce, and people criticized her for it. Their son had been upset about the talk and acted out. Liam could not risk small-town gossip about Nicole, and he couldn't risk her daughter, Katie, being embarrassed like his son had been.

This beautiful grown-up version of Nicole was off-limits.

Chapter Three

Nicole pulled a pecan pie out of the oven, and the kitchen filled with the delicious scents of caramelized sugar and toasted nuts.

Mimi leaned in for a look. "That looks perfect."

"I'm sorry I invited people for dinner without telling you," she said to her mom.

"You know that it's perfectly fine. The more the merrier." She cocked her head. "What has you so nervous?"

There wasn't a chance in all of the flaming pits of hell that she was going to admit her burning desire for Liam, but redirecting the conversation was easy enough. "I'm just anxious in general. I never expected to be starting over at the age of thirty-seven."

"You have so many people who love you and

are here to support you." She cupped one of her daughter's cheeks. "We all have complete faith and confidence that you will find what is best for you and Katie."

"Thanks, Mom." It was nice to have the love and support, but coming home with her tail tucked uncomfortably between her legs was going to take a while to get over.

"Keep an eye on the food, please. I need to return a phone call before everyone gets here."

Nicole had a feeling she was calling her boyfriend, Joseph Bailey, who'd just left for a monthlong visit with his daughter and grandchildren. It made her happy to see her mom putting herself out there and enjoying life, especially after the cancer scare that she'd had not long ago.

Nicole turned down the burner under the green beans and replaced the lid. Katie's adorable giggle drifted in from the living room where she was watching television. Even on Nicole's darkest days, her child's laughter could sooth her soul.

Needing to set eyes on her sweet little sidekick, she moved to the archway that led into the living room. Katie was on her tummy by the Christmas tree with her chin propped on her hands, and the colorful tree lights gleaming on her shiny brown hair.

"Hi, Mommy. Want to watch *Home Alone* with me?"

"I have to keep an eye on the food, but I'll watch something with you after bath time."

"Okay." She laughed again when one of the bad guys got a face full of feathers.

Before Nicole turned to go, the row of photographs across the fireplace mantel caught her eye. One on the end in a wooden frame was a family photo in front of their two-story log house in Montana. She had the urge to rush across the room and turn it facedown. Instead, she went back to the dinner she was supposed to be watching.

When Jeff gambled away their house and most of their money, it was the catalyst that pushed her to file for divorce. The time had come for her to set a better example for her daughter.

On a Monday morning, she'd given Jeff the divorce papers. He'd promised to do better, and because she really wanted to believe him, she'd agreed to talk more about it that evening. But they had never had that conversation. A few hours later, the accident at the lumber mill had taken his life.

Waiting for the investigation to be finished and to receive the official accident report was agonizing, because until then, the guilt wouldn't leave her alone. The same question repeated in her brain and haunted her dreams.

Had he been so distracted by her request for a divorce that it had led to the accident? A cold shiver ran along her spine and settled like a stone into her stomach.

The doorbell rang at 5:30 p.m. on the dot, reminding Nicole about how Liam liked to be on time or early. She would have to make sure she was never late for work.

"I'll get the door," Katie said from the living room.

Liam's deep voice carried from the front entry to the kitchen as he introduced Katie and Travis.

With one deep breath, she worked her mouth into her best impression of a real smile. She was having trouble remembering a time when her true smile came easily. Lately, she'd been forcing the expression.

"Hope you guys are hungry," she said as everyone joined her in the kitchen.

"We sure are," Liam said. "Since we couldn't contribute anything edible, unless it's store bought, I brought wine." He held up both hands. "One red and one white."

"Thank you." Nicole took the bottles and put them on the counter. "Let's open the red."

"Mommy, can I show Travis that really old video game that was yours when you were a kid?"

She chuckled. "Yes, if you promise to stop using the words *really old*."

Katie giggled and hugged Nicole's waist. "Sorry, Mommy. You're not old."

The kids left the room with Katie chattering away, and it was just the two of them. The man she'd adored from afar for most of her life.

"She's right," Liam said. "You look way younger than your age."

His compliment managed to pull her lips into a true smile. "Thanks. I didn't know you were such a good liar."

"Me? Tell a lie? Never." He broke off a piece of crust from the pie, and she pretended not to notice. "I'm a completely open book."

A man who kept no secrets from her would be a refreshing change of pace.

Once Mimi came back downstairs, they put the food into serving dishes and all five of them gathered around the table.

As usual, Katie had plenty to say, but Travis was mostly quiet, only answering direct questions and keeping his answers short. Mimi and Liam weren't much for gossip, but they did helped Nicole catch up on some of the local happenings. Like Mrs. Jenkins's newspaper column that was—as she had suspected—more gossip than news and a popular music venue and dance hall on the edge of town.

When everyone had their fill of pot roast, mashed potatoes and green beans, Mimi brought over the dessert. "Who saved room for pecan pie?"

"I did," Travis said with the most excitement they had seen from him all evening. His dark eyes widened with is smile, both so much like his father's.

"We also have vanilla ice cream if anyone wants some," Mimi said, and cut a slice for the teenager.

"Yes, please," Travis said.

Nicole had a small piece without ice cream while the guys and Katie had a scoop. Travis even had a second piece of pie, which made Mimi smile to know he was enjoying her cooking.

The kids went back to the "antique" video game, and Mimi shooed her and Liam out of the kitchen with cups of hot coffee and suggested they go out onto the front porch to see the full moon.

A cold front was on its way, so they pulled on their coats before stepping outside. Liam's black leather jacket stretched taut across the broad width of his shoulders, tempting her to hug him from behind and rest her cheek on his back. Instead, she wrapped her fingers around her warm mug. Liam had a physique more suited to chopping wood than sitting behind a computer.

"Why did you come back to Oak Hollow from New York?" she asked.

"A couple of things. When Jane and I were getting divorced, I knew she wanted to take a job in Austin, and since that's only an hour and a half from Oak Hollow, we'd both be close to Travis. And it was time to be closer to my mom. My sisters have moved away with their husbands, and she needs to have someone close by to help her out."

He really was the good guy she remembered. Tall, dark and gorgeous with a side of thoughtfulness. Did he have a hidden dark side or secrets he kept closely guarded the way she did? "So, you aren't editing books anymore?"

"I still am. As an editor, I can work remotely."

"You are a busy guy. Working as an editor and running a bookstore."

"And don't forget parenting a teen who doesn't want to be here." He looked down into his mug for a moment before taking a sip.

She was sad to see him struggling with his relationship with Travis. She and Katie were so close, she couldn't imagine this happening to them, but Katie wasn't a fourteen-year-old boy who had been pulled away from his school, friends and sports teams.

The night sky was overcast, hiding most of the full moon and the stars that were struggling to peek through the dark clouds, kind of like she was doing with her life. Her world had been a storm for years, raging and ebbing but never completely clearing. Over the years, she'd been too embarrassed to admit to anyone that she'd been fooled. Ashamed she'd been so gullible and married a man who had everyone believing he was Mr. Wonderful. Jeff had not been a monster, but he wasn't the nurturing and honest man she'd thought she was marrying.

But it was the bed she'd made for herself, and she'd had to figure out a way to not only sleep in it but also how to make it up each day, keeping a tidy in-order appearance. How long would it take for her to see sunny skies?

After paying for Jeff's funeral, she was almost broke and realized she would have to sell the house that she thought they owned outright because Jeff had inherited it from his parents. But when she tried to sell it, she made an awful discovery. He had used it to pay off debts right before his death, and the new owners were making plans to either charge her exorbitant rent or put it on the market. After that, she had sold most of her furniture and they moved into a tiny one-bedroom apartment just in time to receive the next layer of bad news.

The head pastry chef position that she had expected at the resort in Montana went to the owner's son. The man looked for any opportunity to get rid of her. He knew she was a better pastry chef and that others would soon realize it too.

Needing her family more than ever, she had accepted her mom's gift of plane tickets to Oak Hollow for Christmas. The trip had been what she and Katie had needed, and she had returned to Montana ready to take on whatever came next. On December 28, she'd lost her job completely, citing too much time off between the logging accident, funeral, dealing with losing her house and the trip to Texas. That's when she realized she had no choice but to temporarily stay with her mom long enough to regroup and save money while waiting to hear back about the job applications she'd put in at several resorts.

"Where did you go just now?" Liam asked.

"Whatever you are thinking about has put a crease between your eyebrows." He brushed his index finger across the wrinkled spot.

His simple, barely there touch was enough to make her heart flutter. "I just have a lot on my mind these days."

"What is it that has brought you home to Oak Hollow? Were you just needing to be closer to family?"

The good feelings his touch had produced only a moment ago evaporated with a poof. If only that were the case. This was a question she didn't want to answer, but she'd asked him the same and brought this inquiry upon herself. She had secrets she didn't want to share. Some of which she might never be ready to reveal. How could she admit to having had a sham marriage, being broke and having been fired for the first time ever? Telling anyone about the humiliation of her failures was not going to help anything.

What do I say? Think of something.

Liam set his mug on the porch railing. "Sorry. I didn't mean to put you on the spot. I have a crew coming in tomorrow to do a thorough cleaning in the kitchen so you can jump right into cooking whenever you are ready."

She could kiss him for changing the subject, or just because he was totally kissable. Especially with him standing close enough to catch hints of his herbal cologne on the cold breeze. "I appreciate that. It will save me a lot of time not having to do it myself."

"Are you up for going shopping tomorrow to buy ingredients in bulk for the bistro?"

"Yes, I am. That's a good idea. I'll start making a list tonight. Do you trust me to pick the menu?"

"Absolutely. It's your kitchen now."

But it wasn't her kitchen. Not really. This was just a short-term gig to help out a friend and save some money, because running a kitchen with a staff of zero wasn't exactly the reason she went to culinary school.

She hadn't yet achieved the level of success she'd sworn to Jeff that she would. One of his frequent statements floated through her head.

You wasted that money on culinary school.

She was determined to hear someone say "It's your kitchen now, chef," but in reference to a five-star kitchen filled with a large staff. A place that came with prestige and a salary large enough to once again be a homeowner and take care of Katie.

Chapter Four

On Saturday afternoon, Liam tried to convince his son that it would be fun to go shopping with him and Nicole. Truthfully, he was just looking for a buffer to keep him from slipping into the flirting that seemed to come so naturally when he was around her. Forcing the moody teenager to go would only lead to an unpleasant time for all of them, so he left Travis with his grandmother and then went next door to Mimi's farm.

Before he could make it around the front of his truck, Nicole came out onto the wide, covered front porch and waved. Her dark hair was loose and falling around her shoulders, begging for him to see what it would feel like to bury his hands in her curls. She looked fresh and wholesome in a fluffy pink sweater, jeans and brown suede boots.

"Does Katie want to come with us?" he asked. Nothing wrong with a second try at a child-sized buffer between them.

"No. She's with Mimi checking the pecan trees down by the river." She opened the passenger door, got in just as he did and gave a little shiver.

"You don't want to bring a coat?" he asked.

"It's only the sudden warmth of your truck that made me shiver. I have layers on so I can peal them away one by one as needed. Something I learned while living in Montana."

"How many layers do you have on?"

She smoothed the front of her sweater, and her grin was mischievous. "I'll never tell."

"I could take that as a challenge to discover the truth." He said the words and immediately wanted to kick himself.

Good job. I went less than a minute without flirting.

"I guess you could." She tried to hide her smile behind her hand, but her expressive eyes gave her away.

"When we get there, don't let me forget to have you added to the business account so you can come for supplies, too."

"Okay. Want to hear some of my ideas for the opening day menu?"

"This is going to make me hungry, isn't it?"

"Knowing you, yes, which is why I brought these." She pulled a plastic container from her large purse. The lid came off with a pop, and the cab of the truck filled with the scent of cinnamon and sugar.

His mouth instantly watered. "What did you bring?"

"Cinnamon-sugar-covered doughnut holes." She held the container closer and gave it a little shake.

"You win today's prize for best travel companion." He put one into his mouth, and when the sweetness melted on his tongue, he barely resisted moaning with pleasure. "Do you always travel with home-made pastries?"

"On occasion. Do you think these might be something good to put on the menu? Picture a cup of cappuccino with a plate of doughnut holes with a drizzle or a dipping sauce."

"I like it. What else."

She put the doughnuts in the center console space near the cup holders, right within his reach. "I made a list of some items I think might be good to serve. I can make them all ahead of time and then be free to make appetizers as they are ordered."

"Sounds good. What are you planning?"

"A variety of muffin options like banana nut, cranberry and blueberry streusel, a few different cookies, tarts, individual cheesecakes and pies, and so many other things. We can try out different ones for a few weeks and see what sells best."

"I remember pecan cheesecake sold well." He

grabbed another doughnut and popped it into his mouth.

"Good to know. Cupcakes are always a good seller. I have some creative recipes for layer cakes as well."

"I can't wait to try them." Something in her purse made the sound of wind chimes, and she rushed to get out her cell phone like it was urgent. "Are you expecting an important call?"

"An email." She looked at the phone's screen and then sighed as her shoulders drooped. "I'm waiting to hear back about my job applications. But this is only a sales email from a cooking supplies warehouse."

A sharp reminder that she was not staying in Oak Hollow, and apparently, she was eager to leave.

Thirty minutes later, they arrived at the new big box store that was only thirty minutes from their small town instead of the hour he'd had to travel before. They had added to the long list of menu ideas, and he'd forced himself to put the lid back on the doughnuts.

As they walked from the truck to the store, a gust of cold wind carried the sweet scent of baking, and he wasn't sure if it was the doughnut holes or the woman beside him. He pulled his membership card from his wallet and flashed it at the man working at the entrance of the warehouse store. At the customer service counter, a petite woman with turquoise heart-shaped glasses and bright red lipstick greeted them with a toothy smile. "How can I help you today?"

"I need to add this lovely lady to my membership account, please." He slid his card across the counter.

"No problem. Let's get your wife added."

Nicole gasped quietly, but he'd heard it and wasn't sure what her reaction meant. "We're not married," he said.

"Well, you sure do make a cute couple. Could I see your IDs , please?"

It didn't take long to get her membership card, and then he got a flatbed cart they would need for their large items. As he pushed it back to Nicole, she grabbed the hem of her fluffy pink sweater and pulled it over her head. His breath caught and his chest warmed. Something about seeing her taking off clothing made his imagination flash to her doing that in private, just for him. And in his fantasy, she wouldn't have on a long-sleeved, gray T-shirt beneath.

She glanced up as she tied her sweater around her waist. "What's wrong? Has that cart got a wonky wheel?"

He'd come to a complete stop, and luckily didn't have a line of other customers stacked up behind him, but fantasizing in the middle of a store was a problem he needed to get a handle on immediately.

"No. The cart is fine. I was trying to remember if we brought the shopping list or left it in my truck."

Great excuse, genius. He internally rolled his eyes.

She held up the list. "It's right here."

With a brief lecture to himself about proper public behavior, he started moving again. "Where should we start?"

She fell into step beside him. "The baking supply aisle."

Liam loaded fifty-pound bags of flour and sugar, then chocolate chips, honey and lots of spices. Pecans they did not need, thanks to Mimi's orchard. And come springtime, she would have loads of peaches as well.

"What's next on the list?"

Nicole ran her index finger along the piece of paper. "Baking soda and baking powder. One of each."

"What's the difference between the two?"

"Baking powder is actually baking soda mixed with a dry acid. When it comes in contact with liquid, it releases carbon dioxide bubbles, and that causes baked goods to rise. Baking soda doesn't contain an acid. So, it needs something acidic, like lemon juice, vinegar or buttermilk to work. That chemical reaction is key to adding the lift you want to achieve."

"I've gone forty-one years without knowing that. No wonder I can't cook. Cooking really is science."

"Baking certainly is. But don't feel bad. Most people don't know the difference between baking soda and baking powder."

He made a wide turn to get the large cart around to the next aisle. "I often say that we should try to learn something new every day, and now I have."

"I guess I should learn something new, too. What can you teach me?" she asked.

So many tempting thoughts flashed through his head. "I'll see what I can come up with before we get home."

She laughed softly. "That sounds like something you would've said as a kid. Next, we need to go to the dairy section."

When they stepped into the refrigerated dairy room, Nicole shivered. Without even thinking about what he was doing, he wrapped an arm around her shoulders and rubbed her arm to warm her up. She stiffened, and he forced himself to remove his arm in a casual manner, not wanting her to know all the feelings that were stirring inside him. He'd gotten too touchy-feely for someone who had recently lost her husband. He needed to remember that.

Next onto the cart were eggs, butter, milk and cream. Apples, lemons and other fruit were followed by a whole list of ingredients for the appetizers. They grabbed slices of pizza at the concession stand before loading everything into his truck, covering it all with a tarp and then putting the refrigerated items into a huge ice chest.

On the drive home, he found a radio station that played the music they had grown up with, and that sparked lots of childhood memories they laughed about.

"I always liked coming over to help pick peaches during harvest time," he said.

"My mom said she used to take me out to the orchard in a baby carrier before I could even walk. Apparently, a peach was the first thing I ever reached for."

"I remember being in the orchard when you took your first steps."

She cocked her head to study him. "You would've only been four or five years old. I'm surprised you remember something like that."

He hadn't thought about this memory in a really long time, but it was one that always made him smile. "I remember because I was the one you walked to."

"Really? I've never heard this story."

"I was sitting under a tree eating a peach, and you let go of your big sister's hands and walked to me. Not sure if you were after me or the fruit, but you climbed onto my lap."

"That's such a sweet story. We have a lot of shared history between us."

"That we do." Liam found himself hoping there would be a lot more shared stories and moments between them in the future.

"Once the fruit is ripe this spring, a variety of peach pastries would be great. The bistro could become known for..." Her forehead furrowed as she ran the tip of her tongue along the sharp edge of her top teeth.

"Known for what?"

"For locally sourced fresh ingredients."

Was she thinking the same thing he was? Would she still be in Oak Hollow in the spring or would her "temporary" stay be over long before then? This was another reason he could not get involved in any sort of romantic scenario.

But...if he did write another book, Nicole was definitely going to pop into his head as he created the heroine's character. Watching her made him want to write the book his publisher had been asking for.

Back at Sip & Read, everything was hauled into the kitchen through the back door, and he let Nicole organize it however she wanted. As she arranged the pantry and the cooking utensils, some of the joyfulness he remembered as being part of her personality was reappearing. When she stood in the middle of the kitchen with her hands on her hips, her high cheekbones were accentuated by the biggest smile he'd seen from her yet.

Maybe she'll like it here so much she'll stay to run the bistro full-time.

Sunday morning, Nicole got to Sip & Read before sunrise and let herself in the front door with the key Liam had given her. Because she could set her own rules in this one-woman kitchen, today's uniform of choice was comfy leggings and an Oak Hollow high school T-shirt she'd found in a drawer. And with her not pretty but comfortable white clogs that lots of chefs wore, she was not going to win any fashion awards.

She twisted her hair into a bun on the back of her head, put on her Tiffany blue apron and her favorite play list of upbeat songs. Now, she was ready for a marathon baking day because tomorrow the bookstore would be open. The bistro needed to be ready to serve. That wasn't Liam's request. It was a goal she'd set for herself.

Looking around at the empty bowls and trays, there were so many possibilities. A blank slate she was excited to fill. A Bruce Springsteen song started playing, and she rubbed her hands together. "Time to get baking."

"Can I watch?"

"Oh!" Her heart gave a leap, and she spun to see Liam at the foot of the staircase that led up to his apartment. He was grinning in the way he used to do when they were kids and he'd tease her about one thing or another. "Liam Mendez, how long have you been standing there?"

"I just walked down, so if there was dancing involved, I unfortunately missed it."

If he'd waited a few more seconds before startling her, he *would* have seen her dancing. She was also enjoying the feel of the smile he put on her face. "The dance party comes at the end of the day when the work is done. I hope I didn't wake you up."

"I'm an early riser." He came all the way into the kitchen; his usual jeans were replaced with a pair of soft flannel pajama bottoms and a black T-shirt. "What's on your agenda?"

"The whole shebang. Cookies, tarts, pies and turnovers. I'm saving the muffins for tomorrow morning, so they are extra fresh. Sorry to tell you nothing is ready to eat, yet."

"Maybe I'll get lucky on my next trip through the kitchen." His eyes briefly widened before he rubbed his forehead as if he had a sudden headache, but there was a smile he was trying to hide.

"It could happen." She hadn't had this much fun flirting with someone maybe ever. He got as flustered as she did, and that made it twice as enjoyable. To hide her amusement, she turned to grab a large, metal mixing bowl.

"I'll let you get to it," he said. "I'm going to grab a coffee, and I'll be in my office editing. Let me know if you need anything."

She glanced over her shoulder to make sure he'd really gone and then released a long breath. At least she knew she could still feel desire for a man. If he kept saying teasing things that could be interpreted in multiple ways, she was likely to do something embarrassing. Like offer him the opportunity for both of them to get lucky in his office.

Within a couple of hours, she had cookies cooling, chocolate cupcakes baking and was making lemon tarts.

A stair creaked, and she spotted Travis halfway down the staircase. "Hi, Travis. Want to be my taste tester?"

"Sure." He came down the rest of the way a bit faster, but still had his hands shoved into the front pockets of his jeans.

She pointed over her shoulder to the tray cooling on the counter. "I just took brown butter pecan cookies out of the oven. There're still hot so be careful."

"I've never had those, but I like pecans." He scooched one to the edge of the tray with his pointer finger and then picked it up.

"I know. That's why I picked that recipe for today." She smiled at the memory of Travis devouring two pieces of pecan pie after dinner on Friday night.

"How'd you know I like pecans?"

"You seemed to enjoy my mom's pie the other night."

"Oh, yeah," he said around a mouthful of cookie. "What are you making now?"

"I'm working on lemon tarts, and then up next will be key lime bars."

"These cookies are really good. Better not let dad taste them. He'll eat all of them."

"I'll keep that in mind." The way Liam was built, tall and toned and perfect, she couldn't believe he did much overeating.

"Want to help bake?"

"Okay."

"Tuck your hair up into your ball cap, wash your hands and put on one of those aprons."

Nicole got him started on cutting and juicing key limes. "Do you bake with your grandmother?"

"Sometimes. Abuela made a lot of stuff for Christmas. My favorite are her sopapillas."

"Oh, yes. Those are delicious. I'll have to ask her if she'll teach me how to make those and her tres leches cake."

"She also makes something with cream cheese in the center, but I can't remember what they are called."

After she got the tarts into the oven, they made

the key lime bars and she talked him through mixing up a batch of sugar cookies while she sliced apples for turnovers.

Travis was having fun using the stand mixer when Liam came into the kitchen. He'd changed into jeans and a pair of cowboy boots that gave him a rugged appearance she liked. She wondered when he had come back through the kitchen to go upstairs and change clothes and how she'd missed it.

"Looks like you've found yourself a helper," he said, and reached for a pecan cookie.

"I sure have. He is doing a great job."

Liam bit, chewed and then looked at the cookie. "What is this amazing creation?"

"Told you so," Travis said to her.

"Brown butter pecan. How are there going to be any left for the customers with you two living upstairs?"

They looked at one another and shrugged.

"Looks like we will need another batch of those before the bistro opens. Want to help, too?" she asked Liam.

He shook his head and took a step back. "You don't want me helping. I'll mess something up."

"You just need a few lessons."

"You want to give me cooking lessons?"

A quiver started in her stomach. If he took her up on the suggestion, that would be more time spent together while trying to resist him, but she couldn't withdraw the offer now. It was out there, and she'd just have to control herself. "If you own a bistro, you should know at least a little bit about cooking and baking."

He shuffled one cowboy boot on the floor. "Thanks, but I don't think so."

Rather than relief that she'd gotten out of it, Nicole was sad that he'd declined her offer.

"Dad, take the lessons. Please. My stomach begs you."

She forced a chuckle to cover her disappointment.

Liam's cell phone rang in his pocket. "I've got to take this call." He spun and went back toward his office.

"The dough is mixed," Travis said.

Nicole stopped worrying about why Liam didn't want cooking lessons and set aside the measuring cup she'd been using. "Now we divide it into four pieces, wrap them in plastic wrap and chill them."

He followed her example and then put the dough in the walk-in cooler. "If it's okay, I'm going upstairs now."

"Of course. Thank you for the help, Travis. Come bake with me anytime you want. Cutting out the sugar cookies is fun too."

"Okay. I will." He grabbed one more cookie on his way to the stairs.

She glanced toward the swinging kitchen door Liam had gone through. He seemed to be working hard to get out of lessons. But why? Did he hate cooking that much, or did it have something to do with her?

Chapter Five

The sun was just peeking over the horizon on a cold Monday morning, when Nicole arrived at the bookstore to bake fresh muffins. Mrs. Jenkins had written an article in the Oak Hollow Herald about the Sip & Read Bistro reopening—thanks to the return of a hometown girl. She was unusually nervous about living up to the added hype. This was where she had grown up and she wanted, no needed, to impress. They had to know that she'd made something of herself.

But did everyone believe she had given up and was staying here forever?

By the time the front doors opened, everything was artfully arranged, and there was nothing more that she could do. It wasn't normally part of her job to stand out front and serve what she'd baked, but she wanted to see the customers' reactions firsthand.

On one end of the coffee bar nearest the bakery case were three glass-domed stands displaying the fresh muffins: cranberry, blueberry streusel and banana nut. Inside the large two-tiered bakery case, each key lime bar was topped with a curl of lime rind, the cupcakes' swirls of buttercream frosting were decorated with either a sugared edible flower or candied pecan. Within minutes of Liam flipping the Open sign, there was a line of customers ordering coffee and selecting pastries.

Mrs. Jenkins was one of the first to arrive with a group of ladies, most of whom Nicole knew. They tried out everything she had to offer, were full of compliments and promised to write glowing reviews.

Nan Curry—one of the town's oldest residents and award-winning quilt maker—came in with her grandson, Chief of Police Anson Curry and his daughter, Hannah. This spunky little girl was not letting Down syndrome slow her down one bit.

Nicole came out from behind the bakery case and hugged Hannah. "Hello, sweetie pie. You look so pretty today."

"Tank you. Look at my new boots." She tapped one foot to show off her shiny, black patent-leather boots.

"I love them." She smiled at Anson, who had

been a classmate of hers and was still as handsome as he'd been in high school.

"Good to have you home, Nicole," he said.

"Thanks." She wanted to say "it's good to be here," but she didn't want to lie. Instead, she turned to Nan and kissed the woman's soft wrinkled cheek. "How have you been?"

"Just dandy. Now, I've got two great-grandchildren in the house to keep me active and feeling young." She'd had a stroke a few years back, but with the help of Hannah's playful spirit, she had found the will to recover and once again had the prettiest garden in town.

"You got cookies?" Hannah asked, her blond pigtails swinging in opposite directions as she bounced on her toes.

"We sure do. Do you have a favorite kind?"

"Chocit chip." She turned in a circle with her arms out and then pointed to the door. "Look, there's Momma."

Tess Curry looked beautiful in an emerald green sweater dress and was pushing a blue-and-white baby stroller through the bookstore to the bistro counter. She'd come to town as a single mom when she and her daughter, Hannah, temporarily moved to Oak Hollow, and then she ended up married to Anson. She had a wide, dimpled smile, wavy brown hair and owned the antique store on the other side of the town square.

"Welcome home, Nicole."

"Thank you. You have an adorable new family member since I've seen you."

"We sure do. This is Samuel Anson Curry, but we call him Sammy." Tess kissed her husband's cheek and flashed her deep-dimpled smile when he put his arm around her shoulders.

"He's my baby brother. Isn't he cute?" Hannah giggled and leaned into the stroller to kiss his bald head. He grabbed his big sister's hand and cooed to her.

"The absolute cutest ever," Nicole said, and squatted down to smile at the precious baby boy. She wished Katie had a sibling, but she hadn't wanted to have a second child for Jeff to ignore.

They chatted for a few more minutes until Amy motioned her over to the bakery case.

"We are out of the brown butter pecan cookies."

"I have more." The ones she'd hidden from Liam and Travis. "I'll bring them out." Nicole went into the kitchen to refill a tray. She couldn't stop smiling and was so glad she had overprepared, baking way more than she thought they would need, but even still, it was going to be cutting it close. This day was special, and it wouldn't be this busy every day, but it was a nice bump to her ego.

When she went back out to the cafe counter with the tray of cookies, she barely had time to hand it over to Amy before Jenny McKnight, the niece who had been raised as her sister, rushed forward to hug her.

"I'm so glad you've moved home. I'm sorry we weren't here to greet you when you arrived, but we didn't know you were coming."

"Don't even worry about it. I've kept way busier than I ever expected."

"So I've heard." Jenny tucked her dark hair—that looked so much like Katie's—behind her ear. "I can't believe you got the bistro up and running so quickly."

"It's been a whirlwind, but it's kept my hands and my mind occupied."

"We need to make time to hang out and talk soon." Jenny squeezed her hand and lowered her voice. "I want to hear how you are *really* doing."

Her stomach clenched. Jenny knew more than anyone else about her ups and downs, but she didn't know everything. No one did. "Call me tonight and we'll make plans. Did you have a good vacation?"

"It was wonderful. I even managed to get a bit of a tan while sitting by the pool."

"Where are Eric and Lilly?"

Jenny pointed to the children's section of the bookstore and then motioned for her family to join them. Eric, who was taller than everyone else in the store, had their daughter Lilly on one hip, and it always surprised Nicole to see how his smile transformed him from imposing to friendly giant.

"Good to see you again so soon, Nicole."

"You, too." She hadn't expected to see any of them barely two weeks after their Christmas together.

Lilly leaned in her daddy's arms to hug Nicole.

"Hello, precious girl."

"Auntie Nic. Where's Katie?"

"She's at school, but she'll be home in a few hours, and she is going to be so excited to see you. Do you all have time to stay and eat something?"

"That's what we came for. And to see you of course," Eric said, and flashed one of his grins that made women swoon.

She served a strawberry cupcake to Lilly and an apple turnover to Eric and got them seated at a table.

Jenny followed Nicole back into the kitchen so they could talk while she worked. "Our book club meets here tomorrow evening, and you need to join us."

"I'd love to. How big is the group?"

"With you, there will be six of us. You know Tess Curry, and you met Alexandra Walker and Jessica Carter at my wedding. Jessica is now married to Officer Jake Carter. And our fifth member is Emma."

Nicole had known Emma her whole life and used to babysit her back when she was a teenager. Now, Emma and Jenny were business partners at their dress shop on the other side of the town square, where they combined vintage finds along with Jenny's one-of-a-kind clothing designs. Her mom and Jenny had gotten the gene for sewing, but Nicole had zero talent with fabric. All of her skill lay with cooking and baking.

"I won't have time to read whatever book you are discussing and can't promise I won't get pulled away to the kitchen a time or two, but I'll be there."

"Excellent. I know you're busy, and I'll get out of your way, but I hope when we have time alone that you plan on talking to me about what's really going on with you."

"Of course." But she didn't mean it. What was the point in Jenny knowing things that couldn't be changed.

The rest of the day was a whirlwind of greeting people and accepting compliments, especially around lunchtime when they started serving appetizers.

By the end of the bistro's first day, Liam could see the exhaustion in the way Nicole held her body, but it couldn't cover the excitement that was clear on her pretty face. Watching her in her element fascinated him and made him even more hopeful that she might change her mind and decide to stay in Oak Hollow.

He found Nicole in the kitchen getting one of his newest employees up to speed on how the bistro ran. Danny, was in his early twenties and had close-cropped black hair with a design of swirls shaved along each side of his head. He was tall enough to reach the top of all the bookshelves, which came in very handy. Danny started washing dishes, and Liam got Nicole's attention. "I bet you are going to sleep well tonight."

"For sure. I'm exhausted but too amped up to even think about sleeping yet." She bent to put a stack of clean trays on a shelf.

"That's good, because we need to celebrate. Before you go home, can you come upstairs with me? There's something I want to share with you."

She did a double take and touched her throat as if he'd said something suggestive. "Sure. I have time right now."

What was she thinking that made her react that way? She followed him up the dark wood staircase that hugged the back wall of the kitchen. As they stepped through the doorway of his apartment, they were greeted with the sounds of Travis playing a video game in his bedroom.

"You've got some really cool eclectic furniture in here."

"Thanks. A lot of it came from Tess's antique store just a few doors down from here."

The open concept living room, kitchen and dining room combo had one outer wall that was exposed red brick like down in the bookstore with sections still partially covered with plaster.

They crossed through his apartment and then up another small flight of stairs to the rooftop of the two-story red brick building that had been built in 1920.

"Oh, wow." Nicole turned in a slow circle. "What a wonderful spot you've created. I have seen the ivy-covered trellis from the street but had no idea all this was up here. I figured it was hiding the air-conditioning and heating units." There was a trellis on three sides with ivy twined throughout, to give privacy from the town square below.

"Not a lot of people know what I've done up here." The once empty rooftop now had a gas firepit in the center that was surrounded by seating, a couple of lounge chairs and plants. There was a little side table that looked like a tree stump. A wrought-iron table for four was in one corner surrounded by potted plants, hanging baskets and a small water feature of smooth river rocks.

All day, Liam had debated whether or not to bring her up here for a celebratory toast because he didn't want her to get the wrong idea. But what was the wrong idea? What did he think was going to happen? A recent widow who'd been his lifelong friend and wasn't staying in town was not an option for a romantic relationship. He suddenly wished they'd stayed in closer contact over the years, because what he did know about her husband wasn't great, and he got the feeling she was not grieving his loss as much as he'd first thought.

There was a bottle of champagne on ice and two glasses on the little side table between the lounge chairs, and he reached for it. "We need to toast to a reopening more successful than I ever imagined."

"It turned out better than I expected, too." She took a seat on one of the loungers with the green cushions and crossed her feet at the ankles. "Don't expect every day to be like this. The sales will taper off once the new wears off."

"I know, but I think you've made some customers for life. Lots of folks will be coming back for more of your baking." He lifted the bottle of champagne from the ice bucket, held it out in front of him, and with his thumbs pressed against the cork, it popped into the air and landed in a hanging basket.

"Nice shot," she said and applauded.

He poured two glasses and held his up. "To a successful reopening of the Sip & Read Bistro."

She clinked her glass to his. "I'll drink to that."

He reclined back on the other lounge chair. "If you ever need to get away from the kitchen or just have a break, you are welcome to come up here. When it's sunny that umbrella opens to give you some shade." He pointed to a freestanding tan umbrella that opened with a crank handle.

"I appreciate that. You've created a wonderful private oasis right in the center of town."

"Since you get up and start baking so early, you can also come up to the apartment for a nap whenever you want."

"Thanks. I might take you up on that offer." She sipped her champagne and smiled. "Everyone is giving me credit, but we did this together. We got the bistro cleaned, stocked and producing in record time."

"Your pastries need a word that sounds better than producing."

"How about the word *baking*?" she said with a wide smile.

He laughed. "That works."

"Here's to a great partnership." She clinked her glass against his once more. "We make good partners."

He paused with the rim of his glass against his lips and stared up at the stars. The idea of being partners with Nicole made sparks fire off in his brain.

A partnership?

Liam liked the sound of that. Maybe she was starting to see the potential in staying in Oak Hollow and running the bistro. She'd see that she didn't have to go across the country to be successful.

If she stayed… He could consider exploring a relationship that went beyond their reemerging friendship. But did she want to explore the sexual tension bouncing between them, or was he the only one feeling the desire?

Chapter Six

Another successful day at the Sip & Read Bistro was in the books. Nicole had started training a third employee to help out in the kitchen. Now, Amy, Danny and Tina would be able to help with preparing appetizers and other needed prep and cleaning. She hadn't seen much of Liam today and had actually been avoiding him.

One word kept replaying in Nicole's head.

Partners.

Why had she made the comment about them being partners last night? Why couldn't she have said that they made a good team instead of using a word that sounded like she wanted a stake in his business. She couldn't have him thinking she was staying in Oak Hollow instead of going ahead with her career plan. She should have explained what she meant at that moment, but she had hesitated while trying to interpret his reaction, and now, if she brought it up it would become an even bigger deal. It was best to just let this minor worry go, but that would require her to stop overthinking it.

She stepped into the walk-in cooler, which was tucked under the highest part of the stairs, and paused for a moment to breathe in the cold air.

All last night she'd worried that he would take what she'd said as her trying to push her way into his business. She was not. Maybe she should remind him once again that she was only here temporarily. She loved working here with Liam, but it was only a layover on her journey to building a career she could be proud of.

Nicole put the cream away and came back out into the kitchen with the cheddar cheese. She knew deep down that it was a lot more than one word that had her so worked up.

I'm stressing for no reason. I need to let it go. He knows I'm only here temporarily.

"Is this how the charcuterie board should look?"

Amy's question pulled Nicole back to what she was supposed to be thinking about. "Yes. That's perfect." She picked up the appetizer she'd had Amy prepare for book club. "Remember, I'll just be up front if you have questions or need me for anything. Don't hesitate to come get me."

The young girl adjusted her apron. "Got it. Thanks for teaching me."

"You're welcome. I'll show you some more tips and tricks tomorrow."

"Cool. I'm starting to think I might want to go to culinary school in a few years. I know it's expensive, so I'm going to start saving up with my next paycheck."

"Good for you. I'll be happy to share my experience with you and give you some advice."

"That would be amazing."

Could she get Amy up to a point where she could run the bistro alone? She could teach her to make muffins and cookies and some of the other items, but the more complicated pastries might have to be dropped from the menu. There was a lot that would be different once she got a job and left town.

She had prepped as much as she could and left the kitchen in Amy's hands and found Jenny at a table in the romance book section. Emma was walking over from the front door. Hugely pregnant and glowing from her shiny blond hair to her rosy cheeks, the little girl she'd once babysat was now a wife, mother and ran a successful business.

"Hi, Nicole."

"Look at you. So beautiful and glowing and happy." She hugged Emma and the baby gave a strong kick against Nicole's stomach, making her laugh. She put her hand on Emma's belly and got a few more kicks. "I think someone else wants to say hello."

Emma's green eyes tipped up at the corners with her smile. "I'm so ready for her to meet everyone. I'm a few days away from my due date, and it can't come fast enough."

Jenny pulled out a pink velvet covered chair. "Sit down, Em. I saved the comfy chair for you."

"Thank you. I won't argue with that." With one hand cradling the underside of her belly, she eased onto the chair.

Nicole sat across from the other two women. "I stopped by the dress shop to see you, but they said you were home resting."

Emma smiled and lovingly rubbed her baby bump. "I can't be on my feet all day and I've had to take it easy lately. Well, as much as I can with a toddler at home."

Nicole knew the story of how Emma had helped a clueless single dad who'd opened an art gallery next door to her shop and ended up marrying him and adopting his baby boy. "How is little Jax?"

"The sweetest thing ever. He and his daddy are hosting dads' night at our house."

"What exactly is involved in dad's night?" Nicole asked and poured herself a glass of red wine.

Jenny chuckled. "While we meet for book club, all our husbands get together with the kids. We've joked about setting up a camera to see what goes on."

Emma took a sip of the sparkling water Jenny had ordered for her. "It's five guys, two seven-year-olds, a five-year-old, and three kids under the age of two."

Nicole's smiled along with them but felt a pinch in her chest. That is something Jeff never would have even considered doing. Taking care of their child had been *her* department. "Hey, a recording of dads' night could lead to a reality TV program, or at least some good laughs."

"Knowing our crew, that's highly likely," Jenny said.

Next to arrive was Tess, who had walked over from her antique store. Her wavy brown hair was swept back from her face with a tortoiseshell head-band.

The rest of the book club arrived shortly after that. Alexandra Walker was another out-of-town visitor who ended up married to one of the small-town police officers, Luke Walker. He was another one of the longtime residents she'd babysat many years ago. Alexandra was an artist and musician who now worked as an art and music teacher at the middle school. She was mother to a baby girl and her husband's seven-year-old nephew, Cody.

Jessica Carter, another officer's wife, was the town veterinarian and ran the wildlife rescue that Katie was dying to go visit. She was tall with waist-length dark hair and a bubbly personality.

Emma pushed the bottle of wine closer to Jessica. "Drink a glass for me. I miss wine."

Jessica's smile widened. "I won't be having any wine tonight or any other night for months."

"Oh, my gosh! You're pregnant?" Emma asked and reflexively clasped her own stomach.

"Yes, I am." Jessica's quick smile easily gave away her excitement.

There were congratulations, a toast with a combination of alcoholic and non-alcoholic beverages and the conversation turned to her pregnancy announcement. There was so much going on in the lives of these woman that the week's book did not even get discussed. But they raved about the sampler of Nicole's desserts and there were plenty of laughs and stories about their rapidly expanding group of children.

Toward the end of the evening, Emma came back from the bathroom with a mixture of panic and excitement on her face. "Somebody grab my phone from the side pocket of my purse, please. I need to call Nick. My water just broke."

They all jumped up and started talking at once.

They got Emma out onto the sidewalk just as her husband pulled up to the curb.

Nick hopped out and rushed around to the passenger side to help his wife into the car. "Tess, I left Jax with Anson. Are you okay with keeping him for the night?" Nick asked.

"Of course. Call us if you need anything."

"I'll meet you at the hospital in a while," Jenny said.

They all waved as the couple drove off to turn their family of three into a family of four. The other ladies said good-night, but Nicole stood there staring out the front windows.

Discovering her husband's true character shortly after giving birth had been crushing. Once she had a baby who needed so much of her attention, things had changed. She had envisioned the three of them cuddled together, with the new parents happily staring at their little miracle, but he had rarely even held his newborn. With her hormones all over the place, she'd cried now and then, and Jeff had made her feel ashamed and weak. If she had told him that he was the reason she was crying—and not her perfect sweet baby girl—it likely would have been worse.

Jeff had never been unkind to their daughter; he was just for the most part absent from her daily life. If he had even once been physically abusive with either of them, she would have walked out the door immediately. She probably should have anyway. But hindsight…

Nicole checked on the staff in the kitchen and then found Liam in his office.

He instantly closed his laptop the second she walked in.

That of course made her want to know what he

was hiding. It was a leftover anxiety from having to worry about such things for years, and she needed to find a way to get past such fears. It was none of her business what he was working on. "You missed all the excitement. Emma went into labor."

"Oh, wow. Is she okay?"

"Yes. Excited but understandably nervous." She sat in the chair across from him. "Her husband came to get her, and they are on the way to the hospital."

Liam raised his arms high above his head, flexed his fingers and rolled his neck from side to side. "I think I'm done in here for the day."

"Were you working on bookstore stuff or editing?"

"Book stuff."

That answer was vague and could technically be applied to either question, and it made her wonder even more about what he was working on.

Chapter Seven

In a steady rhythm, Liam's running shoes made a shooshing sound on the dirt path and even in the cold morning air, sweat was running down his torso. A slight breeze made the bare-limbed trees rustle and sway. His twice weekly morning runs were not going to be enough if he kept eating Nicole's pastries at the rate he was currently going. He'd have to talk to Anson and the rest of the guys about reinstating their Wednesday evening runs.

He had left Travis sleeping in on this Saturday morning and jogged over to his mother's house. Lidia Mendez might have gray hair and wrinkles that had been enhanced by her frequent smile, but she was still a firecracker who was active in her church and other organizations around town. The

first thing he noticed as he ran up the long driveway was a tree branch brushing the stone wall on
the north side of the house. That would need to be
trimmed soon.

His childhood home was a rustic river rock
and timber house with touches of Spanish style
throughout. A row of three stone archways led into
a courtyard with a fountain in the center, and a brick
pathway interwoven with moss circled the fountain and led to the kitchen door. The courtyard was
edged with flowerbeds that would be blooming with
flowers and herbs come spring.

He knocked and then opened the red kitchen
door. It took more force than usual because the
wood had swelled, so he made a mental note to
come back and fix it when he came to cut the tree
limb. "Hi, Mama."

"Mijo, I'm so glad you've come over." Turning
from the sink surrounded by a colorful backsplash
of ceramic tiles from Mexico and butcher-block
countertops, she dried her hands.

"I can't stay long, but just wanted to pop in and
see if you need anything." He wiped his sweaty
forehead on the long sleeve of his T-shirt.

"I'm always glad to see you, but don't feel like
you have to check on me," which was what she always said. She handed him a clean dish towel and
filled a glass with water. "Where is Travis?"

"He's still asleep. Teenagers and Saturday mornings aren't a good mix." He kissed her cheek and then gulped down half of the water, letting it cool his parched throat.

"Travis is a good boy. He has a good heart, just like you."

"He has been helping out in the bistro's kitchen, and I didn't even ask him to. He took the initiative." Liam finished off his glass of water.

"That's nice to hear. I never could get you interested in cooking. Just like your papa." She patted his cheek in the same way she'd done his whole life. He remembered being small and looking up into her smiling face when she'd bend down to cradle his cheek or kiss his forehead. Now, his petite mama had to reach up high while he looked down.

"Whenever you went on your trips with your church group, Papa always messed up dinner, so we just started going next door to the Winslets' house to eat."

She chuckled. "I know. They told me. Can I make you something to eat before you have to get back to the bookstore?"

"Thanks, but I can't eat and then run back with a full stomach."

The mention of his papa made old memories stir. He'd been eleven when his father got sick and then twelve years old when he became the man of the house, growing up faster than a little boy should. He'd taken on the responsibility of looking after his mom and two younger sisters, knowing that's what his papa would want. Looking after her was a hard habit to break. He wanted his son to be responsible, but he didn't want him to be forced to grow up as fast as he'd had to.

He put his empty glass on the center island's walnut top that he'd helped sand and polish when he'd been about eight years old. "I guess Travis takes after you because he has two parents who aren't good in the kitchen."

With a cup of coffee, she sat at one end of the sturdy kitchen table, another piece of woodworking his papa had crafted by hand. "It's nice of Nicole to let him help. It's also nice to see you spending time with her."

"I don't know how long I'll have her here to run the bistro. She is trying to get a job at a fancy resort, most of which are in other states."

Her amused expression suggested that he was not being honest with himself or the brightest one in the room. "Mijo, I'm not talking about her working for you. I'm talking about something more personal."

"Don't get any ideas about matchmaking."

She picked up her knitting from the table and smiled. "That girl has adored you since she was little."

"What?" His skin felt ultrasensitive, and he sat down hard on one of the high-back kitchen chairs. "Why would you say that?"

"Because it's true. How have you never seen it?"

This was not the conversation he had expected to have with her this morning. "I guess I wasn't that perceptive as a teenager. Before I left for college, she was just a kid to me. Then I rarely saw her."

"And now? How do you see her now?"

He chuckled awkwardly in an attempt to play off his sudden discomfiture, glad his olive complexion didn't reveal a blush. Normally, this topic wouldn't make him so uncomfortable, but something about the woman in question being Nicole—the girl next door—made his body heat in a way that had nothing to do with his exercise routine. But she was no longer the young girl who ran around barefoot. She was mature and funny and more ambitious than ever. And unfortunately, a little sad.

"She's a recent widow, and like I said, she's looking for a job that is nowhere near Oak Hollow, Texas."

"That doesn't answer my question, Mijo. Are you trying to convince me or yourself that you don't see her as a beautiful, smart woman?"

"Anyone can see that she is smart and beautiful."

But her question was a good one to ask himself. Later. He saw Nicole in new ways he didn't even want to think about in present company. As much as he wanted to explore new feelings for her, he couldn't for several reasons. Number one was the widow situation, especially in this small town where it could lead to gossip. He couldn't have Katie embarrassed the way Travis had been when his mom started dating before their divorce was final. People had talked, and his son had overheard.

A big part of holding himself back was self-preservation. Nicole was very career driven and that was fine, but he'd been there and done that with his ex-wife. He didn't need to have another woman walk away from him and their relationship for her career that she valued above their family life.

From the wall beside the oak hutch, the yellow telephone with a long curly cord began to ring. "I'm going to get going so you can answer that."

"I love you, Mijo."

"Love you, too."

He went out the kitchen door, through the courtyard and started at a slow jog. His mom's words about Nicole always adoring him continued to play in his head as he picked up the pace and once again took the trail that wound around and came out a few blocks from the town square.

When Nicole got nervous and jumpy, he put it off to all she'd recently been through, but was it more than that? Was it because she liked him as more than an old friend? He knew she didn't dislike being around him, but was she having as hard of a time as him? He'd been trying to convince himself that she only wanted to be his friend because that helped him keep his desires in check. Helped him hold back from a relationship that he figured would end with someone getting hurt.

But… Nicole *was* the one who mentioned that they made good partners. He came to a complete stop beside a large oak tree and rested a hand on the rough bark.

What if they could work out a deal for partial ownership of the bistro? Would that be something that would tempt her to stay?

All day, Liam thought about what his mother had said about Nicole.

The first week of the bistro's reopening had been a good one, not just for the food but also the books and merchandise up front. After a long Saturday, he flipped the sign on the bookstore's door to Closed. He followed the sound of Nicole's and Katie's voices to a table in the mystery section. Along with the books were a selection of games like Clue and movie boxsets of *Murder, She Wrote* and *Sherlock Holmes*. Now that they were serving food again, he had once again put out a menu on a metal stand with suggestions to pair with the book genre. The menu suggested merlot or cabernet wine, and killer caramel brownies or death by chocolate mousse for dessert.

They were seated at an antique drop-leaf table, and Katie was doing homework while Nicole wrote in her red, leather-bound recipe book. Their sweet smiles made something warm inside his chest.

"Are you doing homework on a Saturday night?" he asked the little girl.

"It's writing, so it's fun homework. I'm writing a story about moving to Oak Hollow. Maybe I should have you read it before I turn it in. That's what you do, right? Help make stories better?"

"It is, and I'd be happy to look at your story," he said.

Katie grabbed her mom's hand across the table. "You should have him look at your book writing, Mommy."

That surprised Liam, and he sat on one of the empty mismatched antique chairs. "You're writing a book?"

She shrugged and wouldn't meet his gaze. "Yes and no. It's just me getting an idea out of my head. I'll probably never show it to anyone."

"Why not?"

"Because I don't know what I'm doing."

Leaning back in his chair, he crossed his arms over his chest. "That's the way every writer starts. You have an idea in your head and need to get it out. Then you figure out how to write along the way."

"It's probably no good."

He really wanted to see her writing. It might give him a peek into her thoughts and the things he knew she was keeping inside. If he had a better idea of what all she was dealing with, he might find a way to make her smile and laugh more, because both of those things gave him joy. "I'll make a deal with you. I'll help you with your writing and you help me with cooking."

Katie climbed onto her knees in the chair. "Do it, Mommy. Then we can put your book on the shelf right here in this bookstore."

"I agree," Travis said as he walked up to join them at the table. "Do whatever it takes to get him to take cooking lessons. I'll even do extra chores if it will help him not torture me with his meals."

"Son, you like to exaggerate as much as I did at your age." Liam messed up his teenager's hair, which made Travis roll his eyes. Seemed like just last month he'd been eager to hold his daddy's hand, but he was growing up and it wasn't unexpected for his son to want some independence. By his age, Liam had already been the man of his house—two years younger than his son's fourteen years.

Travis turned the remaining chair around and sat in it backward with his arms resting on the antique chair's scalloped back.

Nicole smiled at the teenager, entertained by the playful moment between father and son. "Okay. It's a deal." She pointed a finger at Liam. "But you can't laugh at me or my story."

"I wouldn't make a very good editor if I did that."

"I suppose that's true."

"Unless you are writing a comedy?"

"No. It's more of a drama, but it does have the

potential to become a romantic comedy." She closed her recipe journal and put in on the table beside her cup of hot tea. "It was a good day in the bistro. We sold out of some items, and everyone loves the cherry tarts as much as you two. Of course, I haven't found anything y'all won't eat," she said in a smooth transition to a new subject.

"If you make something with licorice, I'm definitely not eating it," Liam said, and grimaced at the thought of that flavor.

"Not much chance of that. How were things up at the front of the bookstore?" she asked.

"Your cooking is definitely bringing people in for repeat business. It was a busy day for book sales as well."

"That's good news." She flicked her pen between her fingers, making it tap rapidly on the table. "I've been looking over sales for the bistro to see what I need to make more of and what I should drop from the list."

"Do not even think about dropping the pecan cookies from the menu."

"I agree with Dad," Travis said.

"I wouldn't dream of getting rid of your favorite cookies," Nicole said, and pressed a hand to her heart. "Promise."

Travis shifted in his chair and bounced his knee in a way that Liam knew meant he was trying to figure out how to ask for something. "What's up with you, Trav?"

"Maybe I could have a part-time job and I can help make those cookies and other stuff after school or on weekends?"

He was pleasantly surprised his son was taking the initiative and asking for a job instead of for the money. "That is a great idea, as long as Nicole is okay with it."

"Absolutely," she said. "I would appreciate the help."

Travis sat up straighter with a big smile. "That's cool. I want to save some money for some camera equipment."

"I want a job, too." Katie got up and was walking in a circle around the table.

Nicole covered a yawn then rubbed her eyes. "How about we call it getting an allowance and you have a deal?"

"Thank you, Mommy." She paused long enough for a quick hug and then continued circling.

He and Nicole shared a smile and high-fived. They knew what the other was thinking without even saying a word. They were doing pretty good in the parent department. At least for today.

"I'm planning to get a few things baked tomorrow. So, if anyone wants to work or get a cooking lesson, you can join me."

Liam admired her work ethic and drive, but he

didn't need her burning herself out. "Don't you ever take a day off? You three are going to get me in trouble for overworking employees and child labor."

Nicole chuckled and then yawned again. "I take days off. Sometimes."

"I suggest tomorrow be one of those rare occasions," he said. "But I think tonight, you need to get some rest."

Nicole blinked a few times. "Are you just trying to get out of a cooking lesson by telling me to take a day off?"

The change in her expression made him worry that he'd upset her. "No. I promise I'll have my lessons. Tomorrow, Travis and I are going to a spot at the river where my dad and I used to fish. It's a short hike from where we park, but not that far and it's pretty. Do you two want to come along with us?"

"I want to go, but Mommy doesn't fish," Katie said. "And I've never fished either. I don't know how."

"I can teach you how to fish," Travis said.

It was such a relief that his son was starting to settle in and not constantly sulking in the apartment. He'd actually come downstairs to find them and hang out and had been smiling more than frowning over the last several days.

Nicole stretched her arms above her head. "I can't promise I'll want to bait a hook or catch a fish, but I would love to go along."

"We also have lures that don't require worms or grasshoppers," Liam said.

"Good to know. Should I pack food?"

"Yes," Liam and Travis said in unison then they all laughed.

He sent the girls home to get some rest, grabbed his laptop from the office and took it upstairs. After seeing how much writing meant to Katie and Nicole, another burst of inspiration had hit him. A new idea was taking shape, and more characters had started revealing themselves. Watching the way Nicole moved and talked and smiled was inspiring him to consider new possibilities. And if he pictured Nicole when he thought about writing sex scenes, that couldn't be helped.

Chapter Eight

Dry winter leaves crunched under Nicole's hiking boots. She walked beside Liam while the kids ran ahead of them, fishing poles swishing through the crisp morning air while they searched for the best spot to stop for a picnic and fishing. She wore a backpack over her pink-and-gray flannel shirt and carried the picnic basket.

In hiking boots, army green cargo pants and a three-tone brown flannel shirt, Liam—who looked like a sexy outdoorsman catalog model—had on a backpack, carried a tackle box and fishing pole in one hand and his free hand swung near her hip. Reaching out to hold it or even just let her arm brush against his knuckles was so tempting that it was becoming a struggle. She shifted the picnic basket to carry it between them as a safety barrier to prevent her from doing something she couldn't take back.

"Let me take that basket," he said. "It looks heavy."

Before she could argue, he had lifted it from her grasp. "Thanks." Now she had to find something to do with both of her hands, so she curled her fingers around the straps of her backpack.

Walking hand in hand was not something she should be thinking about.

They'd renewed their old friendship and developed a new level of connection. It was just what she needed, and she didn't want to mess up a good thing with a fumbling try at romance. She would probably end up doing something embarrassing like kissing him when she read the signs wrong and him being horrified. And what if the real thing wasn't as good as the fantasies that she'd had about him for years? She needed a friend more than a lover. At least that's what she would keep telling herself and see if it stuck.

We are friends. Not in a hand-holding relationship.

"I'm seeing signs that Travis is getting back to the happy kid he used to be. I was worried he'd stay mad until his mom returns in December. I think having you and Katie around has helped."

"I'm glad. Kids just need time to adjust. And we both know Oak Hollow High School can't compete with the school he was attending in Austin."

"Did he tell you about his old school?"

"Yes. While he was helping me bake. Apparently, they have ice hockey, a swim team and the photography and film studies electives that are not offered here."

"And here there's only football, basketball, baseball and track. Since he has big dreams of someday being a filmmaker and professional photographer, I think I'll start looking for someone in the area who can help him with that."

"Great idea. I like that he already has a passion and knows what he wants to do."

"Kind of like you with your cooking. Moving here has been a big change for him. I try to keep that in mind when he starts testing me with an attitude that he knows won't fly with me. And having your mother leave for a year…" He shook his head but didn't finish his sentence.

"I guess she's pretty dedicated to her career?"

"That's for sure." He watched his son with a thoughtful expression, and a touch of sadness in his dark brown eyes. "She pretty much puts her career before anything else."

That sounded familiar. At least his ex-wife was saving lives. Jeff had done the opposite, off losing things like her respect, her love, their money and their house. "Did your ex-wife put her job before family life and your marriage?"

"Yes. She's remarried to a doctor who's on the

trip with her. Apparently, *he* understands the demands of being a doctor."

"I can sympathize with a spouse putting things before family."

"Jeff was in the logging industry, right?"

"Yes, but it wasn't so much his career as having fun. When he wasn't working, he was off with his buddies, not with us." She hadn't meant to give that much away about her marriage, but she wanted Liam to know she understood some of what he had been through.

"I don't want Travis to feel like he doesn't come first for me. I try to make sure we do things like this as much as possible."

"You are a really good father." Why couldn't things have been like this in her marriage? The man Jeff Evans had pretended to be might have gone on family outings like this, but the real man had gone hunting with his buddies most weekends and then to play poker and whatever else it was he did when he hadn't been at work. At first, her suspicions about what all he was doing had consumed too much of her time and energy, but she'd grown numb to it and found a way to let go of that worry.

"We found a good spot," Katie called back to them.

It was time to get her head back into the present and stop worrying about the past. "Is there a flat spot for the picnic?"

"Yep. It's good."

Nicole spread out a blanket from her backpack while the other three got set up for fishing. The calming sound of water rushing and gurgling over the rocky riverbed was a sound that soothed her. A silvery ribbon of water meandered through the Hill Country and was edged with cypress, sycamore and willows. The water was not icy cold like you expect for January or frozen like it would be in Montana. Because the river was spring fed, it was at about the same temperature all year round, and she could reach into a shallow part of the river for pretty pebbles without freezing her fingers off.

When she overheard Travis say he was hungry, it didn't take her long to get the food out and set up on the blanket. Croissant and pita pocket sandwiches, chips, fruit, cheese and pasta salad. For dessert she'd packed cookies, brownies and a thermos of hot chocolate.

"The food is ready whenever you are," she called to them down by the water.

Travis was the first to reel in his fishing line and join her at the blanket. It was sweet that Liam stayed with Katie until she was ready to leave the water's edge. Watching this kind, handsome man with Katie gave her an unusual twang in her chest. She didn't want to risk analyzing it and getting it wrong. If she'd learned anything over the years, it was that she was terrible at judging men and guessing what they were thinking or planning.

Or what they might be hiding from her.

She gave everyone wet wipes to clean their fishy hands and started passing out food.

They laughed and talked about movies and hobbies as they ate.

"You knew Mommy when she was little, right?"

"I sure did. I have known her since she was born."

"That's a long, long time," Katie said. "Tell us some funny stories."

Liam leaned his back against a tree trunk and stretched out his legs. "Let's see. There was one time when we were in the peach orchard and your Mimi was watering some newly planted trees. There was mud and I was making mud pies in a little tin pan, but your mommy was too busy stuffing mud in her diaper."

The kids rolled with laughter, and so did Nicole and Liam.

"Now tell us something funny about Dad," Travis said.

Nicole tapped her chin and looked at the puffy white clouds rolling overhead. "One time we were down by the river behind the pecan orchard. I picked up a piece of wood, and when I realized there was a tarantula on it, I flicked the spider off. It landed on Liam's leg, and he screamed really loud before jumping into the river."

Liam shivered as they all laughed. "I'm still not a fan of large, furry spiders."

"I have another good one about the time he ripped the back of his pants right down the middle and didn't even know it."

"Did you tell him?" Katie asked.

Nicole grinned at Liam. "Eventually, I did." They each told a few more stories, and then they started putting the food away.

"I'm going to get out my camera and see if I can get some photos and videos of animals," Travis said, and stuffed his trash into the bag they'd brought. "Thanks for the food."

"He really takes his photography hobby seriously," she said.

"Don't let him hear you say it's a hobby. He's already looking into the best colleges for filmmaking." Liam grabbed a cookie before she closed the container. "Are you sure you don't want to fish?"

"No, thanks. I'm going to relax and read my favorite book." She held up her well-worn copy of *Her New Life written by the super-secretive author, Ivy Moon.*

Liam stiffened, and the cookie he was holding broke into several pieces and dropped onto the blanket, and he stared at the book in her hand without saying a word.

His odd reaction was curious and made her wonder several things at once. Was it this particular book that had made him suddenly speechless or something else? Being in the publishing industry, he'd no doubt heard of this bestselling romance novel, but why was his reaction so startled? If he had been the one to edit this book, you'd think he'd be happy to see she liked it so much and would admit that it was one he'd worked on.

"Mommy has read that book three times," Katie said. "It's her favorite."

"Three times?" Liam's eyes rounded with surprise.

"It's not a bestseller for nothing. And the mystery surrounding the author makes it even more interesting."

From the first chapter, she'd seen some of herself in the heroine, and as the story unfolded, the character became a model for the strong woman she wanted to become in her real life. The eerie part of the book was the heroine's ex-boyfriend. He was the book version of Jeff. But the ex-boyfriend was the one who sparked the heroine's journey to a new life and her happily-ever-after, and Nicole had set her mind to doing the same. It was this book that had given her the courage to ask for a divorce. If only it had been published a few years earlier.

Liam was still in the same position on one knee as if he'd become stuck in the process of standing up. Finally, he cleared his throat. "Thanks for lunch." He gathered up the pieces of cookie and took them with him as he walked to the water.

Katie skipped along behind him, asking at least five questions before they even got their fishing poles back in the water.

Prickles popped up on her skin. Maybe Liam knew the true identity of the supersecretive author and was afraid she was going to ask him about her?

Now, she was not going to be able to resist trying to get him to tell her.

On the short drive back to Oak Hollow, Liam was more relaxed than he'd been in a long time. He was enjoying himself and wasn't ready to take Nicole and Katie home. "If you girls aren't too tired, what do you think about going back to the bistro and cooking dinner or baking a batch of cookies? I can have a lesson, and the kids can earn some money."

"I'm hungry again," Travis said, and was echoed by Katie's quick, eager response.

"Hey, what happened to my day off?" Her smile told him she was not at all upset about the idea.

"What if the kids and I do all the work and you just sit in a chair and direct us?"

She laughed. "Sounds good to me, but I highly doubt that will happen."

"It's worth a try. What should we have for dinner?"

The kids started yelling out options, many of which they didn't have the ingredients to make.

Once they had all washed up from their day out in nature, Nicole got out a variety of ingredients and lined them up on the prep island. "We are going to make gourmet grilled cheese sandwiches."

"Sounds good to me," Liam said.

"We need cooking music, Mommy."

"We sure do." She pulled up one of the more upbeat playlists on her phone, and it started with a Michael Jackson song. "How's that?"

"Good. Now we have to dance before we cook," Katie announced, and began to do the twist.

Travis backed up until he leaned against the door of the walk-in cooler, his body language clearly stating he had no intentions of joining in on the dancing.

"Hey, wait a minute," Liam said. "You said the dancing came *after* the cooking was done."

"Did I say that?" Her hips swayed to the rhythm of the music, and she giggled the way he remembered her doing as a kid.

"So, I did miss you dancing that first morning you baked?"

"No. I didn't start until you went to make your coffee."

"Not fair." He took her hands and then pulled her into his arms for a quick spin around the center island.

When the first song ended, she got the kids started on buttering the bread, and she taught Liam how to chop carrot sticks without cutting himself. As she had fully expected, she did most of the cooking and they did the observing. But when it came time to eat, she had a feeling they were going to do most of that.

They took their plates upstairs to the apartment because the kids wanted to see the newest episode of one of their favorite sitcoms. Along the red brick wall were most of the kitchen cabinets and the oven. The open concept kitchen had butcher-block countertops, an antique ivory-colored backsplash and decor that told everyone that there were two guys living here.

On the other side of a small breakfast bar was a vintage 1950s' table with chrome metal legs and a white pearlescent Formica top. The chairs were covered with red vinyl, and it felt so familiar to her.

"Was this the table in your breakfast nook at your mom's house?"

"Yes, it is. She moved one of the tables my father built into the kitchen."

"I need to bake one batch of sugar cookies before I go home tonight, and then I can decorate them in the morning. Do any of you want to help?"

"I'm too tired to bake." Katie yawned, and that triggered Travis to do the same. "Can I stay up here and keep watching TV?"

"As long as the guys don't mind us crashing their bachelor pad for a little while longer."

"Fine with me," both of them said with the same inflection and shrug of one shoulder.

"Okay. I'll be as quick as I can."

"I can help you," Liam said. The second the words left his mouth, he realized they be alone together in the kitchen. After their fun day together, it was going to be a challenge to keep himself from flirting or resist touching her.

"The dough is already made and chilled," she said over her shoulder as he followed her down the stairs. "We just need to roll it out, cut the cookies with your choice of cookie cutters and bake them."

"That sounds like something I can handle."

He watched her without being obvious—he hoped—as she moved about with quick efficiency. She got out a ball of dough wrapped in cellophane and a container of metal cookie cutters, and then prepped a spot on the stainless-steel work surface with flour. With the palm of one hand, she pressed the sugar cookie dough down into a thick disk.

"Want to roll it out?" She offered him the wooden rolling pen.

"I think I need a demonstration first."

As she moved the rolling pen back and forth across the dough, her body moved in a sensual rhythm that was doing something to his body that he hadn't felt in a really long time.

Maybe coming down here to do this alone with her wasn't a good idea.

He was now aware enough to recognize there was a mutual attraction between them, but if he let himself cross a line, he'd have a hard time stopping. The faint murmur of the television drifted from upstairs, and he glanced up at the high ceiling. Those two kids had been through enough and did not need to be embarrassed by gossip about the widow who moved on too soon, and with her boss no less.

Maybe that's another reason to consider talking to her about a stake in the bistro. Then I wouldn't be her boss.

Nicole didn't need the added stress of gossip in her life either. He needed to be patient and wait to see if she was really leaving before considering taking things further between them in either business or pleasure.

She set the rolling pen aside. "Okay. Find the cookie cutters you want to use."

He dug around in the container and pulled out a few that looked interesting. "Is this a fishing hook."

She laughed and turned it around in his hand. "It's a candy cane, but we can totally turn it into a fishing hook. I'll use royal icing to decorate it. Find the fish shaped cookie cutter and we will do a batch of fishing themed cookies since that was today's activity."

"Will people want to eat a cookie that looks like a fish?"

"They will be cute enough to eat. I promise. I'll

use fun colors, and they will look more cartoon than realistic."

"I'll trust you on that." Standing shoulder to shoulder, he could feel the heat of her body and smell a subtle hint of vanilla in her hair.

"Start on the edge of the dough and work your way across, keeping the cookies close together so we get as many as possible out of the one rollout."

He messed up the first two cookies he tried to move onto the cookie sheet, but with a demonstration, he got the hang of it. Once a few trays were in the oven baking, they started cleaning up the mess they'd made.

"As soon as the cookies are out of the oven and the kitchen is clean, we are going home so you can do whatever it is you need to this evening."

Liam rinsed the cookie cutters and put them on the drain rack. "For the book festival that we are having in a few weeks, do you think you could make cookies that look like books?"

"Absolutely. I already have a cookie cutter that is an open book, and I can easily turn a square into different book covers. I might even be able to find one that is a typewriter."

"Perfect."

"Tell me more about this book festival."

"It's something I did when I first opened Sip & Read, and now everyone has come to expect it. I have about twenty authors coming to set up tables in the square by the gazebo. Throughout the day some of them will do readings in the store. For the kids, there will be crafts and a few children's authors. There is a husband and wife team coming, and they are really great with kids. She illustrates and he writes the stories."

"How cool that they work together. Are all the authors from this area?"

"A lot of them are from different areas of Texas. A group of five romance authors from San Antonio and one from Austin. A science fiction and historical author are coming from around the Dallas area. A few are coming from out of state. One big name writer, Sara Love, is coming from New York. She is an author as well as an editor for the same publishing house where I work. I've known her for years."

"I've read most of her books and really liked them. I'm excited to meet her."

"I'm glad you didn't say you hate her books."

"Why? Are you Sara's editor?"

"Yes, I am."

"Good thing I didn't say they are garbage. I'll have to be more careful what I say about books and authors from now on."

"Don't edit yourself on my account. Feel free to speak your mind."

"Sara Love's books are good, and they really grab you and pull you in from the first page. Is there any chance my favorite author, Ivy Moon, might want to make her first appearance in our little town?" she asked hopefully.

A cold wave rippled across his shoulders. He couldn't believe how much she was fangirling over that book. "No. You know she doesn't do public appearances."

"That's what I was afraid of. Too bad. I'm always hoping there will be some big reveal they do for publicity or to promote another book."

"Don't hold your breath on that one." He didn't tell her that there wasn't a chance in hell of Ivy Moon making any public appearances.

Chapter Nine

Nicole knocked on the doorframe of the open door to Liam's office. Once again, he immediately closed his laptop as if it held secret information.

Maybe it does.

She would never snoop, but that didn't mean she couldn't wonder what he was doing. She moved farther into his office and braced her hands on the back of a leather high-back chair. "I came to see if you'd like a late lunch."

"Yes, please. How did you know I was starving?"

"Because I am too, and while I was making mine, I made one for you."

"Is Amy watching the kitchen?"

"Yes. She's catching on to everything quickly, and Tina is on her way for her afternoon shift. I'm also happy to report that Danny is a hard worker and eager to learn. He's up at the coffee bar right now."

"Good to hear. Have you already eaten?"

"Not yet."

"Go get your lunch and eat with me."

"I can do that. I'll be right back." She could not allow herself to read too much into him wanting her to have lunch with him. For all she knew, he wanted to discuss the bistro's profits or some other business-related topic.

She carried in a serving tray with two turkey sandwiches and glasses of iced tea right as he was putting a stack of file folders and papers on the floor under his desk. It was the kind of desk with a solid front, so she couldn't tell how much other stuff he had stowed under there. Just knowing there were piles on the floor made her want to get in there and clean and organize his messy clutter.

"I cleared a spot for you."

"Thanks." She set the tray on his desktop beside a brass lamp and an Oak Hollow High School cup filled with pens and pencils.

"I got an email from Sara Love. She has extended her trip to town for the book festival to three nights, but I only have her booked for two nights at the B and B. Unfortunately, they can't extend it to three."

"What about the hotel?"

"It's fully booked because of the book fest and a quilt show going on at Queen's Sew N Sew. I sure wish the old B and B on the edge of town hadn't closed. Hopefully someone will reopen it soon."

"What are you going to do about her last night in town?"

"I guess I'll let her stay in my apartment."

Something unpleasant curled in her stomach at the thought of this woman staying in his apartment, but it wasn't her place to be jealous or say anything. "I have a question. I know there's no chance of my favorite author coming to the book fest, but since you're in publishing, do you know if there will be another book by Ivy Moon?"

Liam coughed as his sip of tea seemed to go down wrong. Once he recovered, he cleared his throat. "I've heard a rumor that she is thinking about it."

"Oh, yay." She clapped her hands. "That's good news." His demeanor had suddenly changed, and she found his reaction very curious. Every time this book or author was mentioned, he got twitchy. Did he personally know Ivy Moon? Had he edited her book but could not admit to it because of the secrecy? An unwelcomed bit of jealousy zipped through her chest. Had they dated?

Do they still date? She internally sighed and put down her sandwich. *I'm being ridiculous. I need to get a grip.*

She studied him, trying to get a better feel for his mood. No one knew anything about the mysterious ultrasecretive author. No photos on her social media, only animated images or caricatures. No interviews or public appearances.

"You know who she is, don't you?"

"What makes you think that?" He focused intently on his sandwich instead of her.

Leaning forward, she propped her elbows on his desk. "Can you give me any hints at all about her? Is she old or young?"

He used a finger to draw an X across his heart. "Sorry. I'm sworn to secrecy."

"So, you do know her." She sat back and observed him with crossed arms and a grin. "Maybe I'll get you drunk and get it out of you."

His lips pressed together as if resisting a smile. "How? Are you going to tickle me until I confess?"

"I might."

"I'm curious. What is it about Ivy's book that you love so much?"

"For one, I can identify with the heroine because…" Nicole had almost said because she'd gotten herself out of a bad situation like in the book, but she hesitated. Saying the wrong thing could give away the dark parts of her life and marriage. She had already told him about Jeff not spending time with them, but that wasn't everything. Some secrets needed to remain a secret.

"She started over. She became successful and happy and found her place in the world like I'm in the process of doing, but I'm still in limbo with where I'm going to land."

She had something to prove not only to the doubters, but to herself. She couldn't let culinary school be for nothing. "I want to have a successful career like the heroine in *Her New Life*."

Liam stomach clenched, and suddenly his last bite of turkey sandwich wasn't going down right. If only he could rewrite Nicole's words and goals as easily as hitting the backspace key on his laptop and rewriting the words he wanted to hear. His mama's comment about Nicole liking him had gotten into his head.

But she didn't like him enough to stick around and have a relationship with him.

Her drive for a "successful" career was too much like his ex-wife. This was a good reminder of why they shouldn't get romantically involved.

"Anything else you like about the book?" he asked.

"I like the dedication. 'To strong women everywhere, even if they don't know it yet.'" Nicole pulled several pins and the tie from her hair, letting her curls tumble around her shoulders. "It is beautifully written. So full of emotions and imagery. The love story is real and raw. The hero is not a knight in shining armor, but he is wonderful, and the heroine is strong and determined and becomes a successful woman. She finds…real love." She looked down and seemed to shrink into herself.

Real love?

Was she sad because she'd had and lost that kind of love with her husband? He had a strong feeling it was a lot more likely that she had not. The guy had been an ass who fooled most people, but he hadn't fooled Liam. They hadn't been close enough during those years for him to interfere in her life, and he hadn't known how to say anything to Nicole about his suspicions. But now he wished he'd talked to Nicole about the conversation he overheard years ago. Maybe it would have helped her in some way.

She glanced at the antique clock on top of a bookshelf, stood and gathered up her plate that still had half a sandwich. "I need to get back to the kitchen."

"Thank you for lunch," he called to her retreating back. "Nic?"

She paused at the doorway and looked back at him. "Yes?"

"I have to take some stuff out to my mom's this evening. Want me to come over and we can work on writing? You can show me what you have so far."

Tipping her head, she bit her lip. "Okay. It's a plan."

There was something going on with her that she didn't want to talk about. And he was dying to discover what was haunting her. What was it that was making her smile not come as easily as it once had?

He pushed his unfinished lunch aside and opened his laptop. He had been working on his book when she came into his office and closed his computer like she could somehow see through the back of the screen to read his words.

After hearing all the flattering and insightful things Nicole had said about the book, Liam was even more inspired to work on his new manuscript. Another new scene was forming in his mind, and the more he typed, the more the plot developed. He let his fingers fly across the keyboard, getting into a writing groove that he couldn't always reach, but he loved it when he could.

His publisher was asking for another book. His fans were asking for another book. And it looked like they were going to get their wish. But now, as he wrote, he found himself wondering what Nicole was going to think about this story.

The sun had already set by the time Liam knocked on Mimi Winslet's front door, and it only took about five seconds before Katie answered.

"Mommy is upstairs in her room writing. Want me to show you where it is?"

"Sure. Lead the way." He waved to Mimi who was sitting on the couch sewing and watching TV.

Katie raced up the stairs and burst into the room without knocking, and Nicole startled with a hand to her heart.

"Katie Cat, we've talked about knocking."

"Sorry, Mommy. Liam is here to help you write better. See you later," she said to them, and closed the bedroom door, shutting him inside with Nicole.

"Where does that girl get all of her energy?" he asked.

"I think she sucks it right out of the atmosphere. Come have a seat." She was sitting cross-legged on one of the twin beds and motioned for him to take the one chair at the small desk.

Instead of sitting on the chair, he sat on the twin bed across from her, separated by the width of the nightstand between them. "For some reason I feel like we are going to get into trouble for being alone in your childhood bedroom with the door closed."

She laughed. "It does feel a little bit like I'm back in high school."

"Did you ever sneak boys into your room?"

"One time a guy climbed the tree outside of my window, but I wouldn't let him come inside."

"Would you have let me in if I had climbed up to your window when you were in high school, and I was home from college?" He couldn't resist asking. He had to know if it was true that she had always liked him as more than a friend. It had been going round and round in his head, gathering speed and spinning into a whole scenario that he wanted to play out.

She was attempting to hide a shy grin. "I probably would have let you come in because… I've always trusted you."

Was that a good thing or a you-are-like-a-brother thing? "Good to know that I'm trustworthy."

She got up and retrieved a stack of pages from the desk along with a red and a blue pen. "I printed out the first chapter. I don't know what color you want to make notes with, or do you need a pencil?"

"Blue works." She was so cute when she was nervous.

"Remember that I have no idea what I'm doing."

"I'm going to tell you the same thing when we're in the kitchen for my next cooking lesson."

"You are a professional and I am a novice." She went back to her open laptop on the bed.

"It's not like you to be this insecure about something." He remembered her being so confident and sure of herself. Had her husband sucked the confidence right out of her?

"If I'm going to do something, I want to do it well."

He took off his boots and reclined on the bed to read. The story caught his attention from the first page. It drew him in and kept him reading, and he was relieved that her writing was good. Even though there were some beginner mistakes, it had heart and a depth of emotion that was hard for most new writers. Thankfully, he would have plenty of good things to say along with his suggestions and corrections. She was too fragile and hard on herself right now. She'd probably be mad if she knew he was treating her with kid gloves, but she needed her confidence built up after years of what he suspected was a man doing the opposite.

He made a few notes along the way and then sat up. "I can already tell this is going to be a great story. I want to know what happens next."

"Really? It has promise?"

"Yes, it does."

She flopped back onto her bed as if she could finally relax, but only a few seconds later, she sat up and held out her hand for the pages. "Can I see the notes you made?"

Instead of giving her the pages, he moved to her bed and sat beside her so they could both see them. "Right here you wrote 'He walked across the room.' That gets the point across. You've told me he did it, but I can't picture the room, or the way he moves."

She sat up straighter and tucked one foot beneath her, making her arm brush against his. "That makes so much sense. Let me work on that and see what I can come up with." She put her computer on her lap and scrolled to the start of her manuscript, typed then deleted then typed again and smiled.

"Did you come up with something good?"

"It is at least better than it was."

"Read it to me," he said.

"'He shoved his hands into the pockets of his

trousers and the hallway light cast his tall, hunched shadow across the leather-bound volumes lining the bookshelves.'"

He clapped. "Nice work. You catch on quickly."

"Thanks. Now that I have someone to bounce ideas off of, this is even more fun than I thought it would be."

"Writing can be very solitary. It's nice to have a critique partner. Or as you said, someone to share ideas with."

She leaned her shoulder against his. "Have you ever thought about writing a book instead of just editing?"

His stomach clenched. "Yes. I've thought about it." He hated that he was being misleading, especially since she was the one who had made him open his laptop and start a new document entitled Book Two.

"I know it's a lofty goal, but I would love to be able to someday write half as well as Ivy Moon. It would be so great to learn from her or just pick her brain. Since you are part of the in crowd, if you do write, you might even be able to have Ivy as your critique partner."

If she only knew. "What would you pick her brain about?"

"One thing would be about how she creates her characters. They are so real. Even though the ex-boyfriend wasn't in much of the book, it's like the author knew me or was tapped right into my life. It's kind of eerie the way I could identify with so much of it. Like someone had a window into my world and spied on my life.

The muscles across his shoulders tightened. How could he tell her he'd written the book she loved and that she identified with it because he *had* "spied" on her life. Not on purpose, but he had stumbled into an overheard conversation. He had based the bad guy on what little he knew about Jeff and written the heroine's story the way he wanted things to work out for Nicole.

Chapter Ten

Katie and Travis came into the kitchen, her daughter full of energy and Travis dragging behind with a sour expression. Since their schools were next to one another, Travis had started walking her to Sip & Read after school. Then they would have a snack and do homework.

"How was your day?" Nicole asked them.

"Boring," Travis said, and let his backpack slide off his shoulder and caught it with his hand before it hit the floor.

"I made a new friend." Katie twirled on one foot, her long brown hair fanning out behind her. "Her name is Susie."

"Oh, good. I knew you wouldn't have any trouble making friends. Your snacks are already on the table."

"Thank you, Mommy."

"Thanks." The teenager followed Katie to the small bistro table in a corner near the base of the stairs, and both children sat down to eat.

"Did you print any of the photos you took while we were at the river?" Nicole asked him.

"Not yet. I'm trying to figure out some new editing tricks. I wish I had my old photography teacher to help me."

Amy, who was working the coffee bar and bakery case, came through the swinging door and handed her the order on a slip of paper. "I need a charcuterie board, please. They want goat cheese. We still have that, right?"

"We do. I'll have this ready in a few minutes."

"Hi, Amy." Katie ran over for a quick hug with the girl who had caught her interest.

"Hey, Katie. Come find me after you do your homework, and you can help me put new books on the shelf."

"Cool."

Amy's pink-tipped blond hair had Katie asking to do the same. Nicole had already ordered clip-on hair extensions in fun colors that would temporarily look nice with her daughter's long dark hair. She planned to surprise her with them on Valentine's Day.

Nicole got out the ingredients from the cooler and started preparing the snack board. Two kinds of cured meats, three cheeses, nuts, olives and a couple of different crackers.

"Where are you going to do your homework today?" she asked the kids. Her daughter thought it was fun to move around to different areas of the bookstore each day.

"I don't have any homework," Travis said. "The stuff they taught today is stuff I already learned in Austin, and I got my homework done at school."

"That's good. Now you'll have more time to work on your photos."

"I have homework," Katie said. "Math and English. I'm going to sit near the children's section so I can make notes after my homework is done because I think it needs a few improvements."

"I was just thinking the same thing," Liam said on his way into the kitchen. "Want to help me work on adding some improvements to that section before the book fest?"

"Really? Yes, I want to help. I'll make a list of ideas after my homework." She crunched on a carrot stick.

Liam winked at Nicole, and it made her pulse flutter at the base of her throat. She was so appreciative of the way he was with her daughter. A real father figure, like Katie had never had.

"I was able to get a few good cookie cutters for the event," Nicole said. "Another book, a typewriter and I also have letters to spell out words or book titles or however we can think of to use them."

"That sounds great."

"I have also started working on a few other dessert and appetizer ideas for the event. I think we will need more food since people will be here all day. Maybe we should offer sandwiches." She held up the finished snack board. "Are you here for this?"

"Yes, ma'am. And now we need an apple pie à la mode. I'll deliver this and be right back."

She started on the next order, and Liam was back before she could finish.

"I forgot to tell you. Guess what is reopening?" he asked.

"I don't even know what to guess. Tell me."

"The old drive-in movie."

"Oh, wow. How fun. We should go." She bit the inside of her cheek.

Now I'm asking him on dates?

"Does that sound fun?" she asked the kids, so he would know she wasn't asking him on a romantic date, even though she liked that idea a lot.

"Yes. I love going to the movies." Katie skipped from the kitchen, with a book and spiral notebook clasped against her chest.

"Sure. I'm going up to the apartment." The teenager trudged up the stairs like he was being punished.

"He seems a little down today," she said to Liam. "You might want to check in with him."

"That's what I was just thinking."

"It might be about missing his photography and film class, but it could be more than that."

"I'll go talk to him after I take this order out." He turned to go but paused. "What do you say to the drive-in movie on Saturday night?"

"Sounds perfect."

Once she was alone in the kitchen, she danced around the center prep island.

They took Nicole's SUV to the drive-in movie theater, and since it was the kids' first time, they let them sit in the front seat so they would have a good view of the movie screen. Nicole now found herself in the back seat with Liam. In the dark. Something she'd thought about a time or two, or two thousand. Especially when she'd loved him from afar from about the time she was aware of boys not having cooties. They had been alone in her bedroom joking about being teenagers and now they were together in the back seat at the drive-in. The desire to cuddle was making her jumpy. All she wanted to do was get close enough to breathe in his scent, but their children were in the car.

"Dad, did you eat all the Junior Mints?" Travis shifted in the driver's seat to look at them.

"I believe I did, son."

"But the movie hasn't even started. Can we go get more and some popcorn?" Travis asked.

"Sure." Liam pulled out his wallet and handed

his son some cash. "I'll take a Coke, please. Nic, what would you like?"

"I'll have the same."

"Wait for me." Katie scrambled out of the car and hurried after Travis.

"I hope he doesn't mind that she follows him around like a puppy."

"You mean just like you used to do to me?" He rested his arm across the back of the bench seat, much like a teenager might do when they wanted to put their arm around a girl but were too shy.

Too bad that wasn't the case with Liam. "Did I really do that?"

"Yes, ma'am. Katie reminds me so much of you at the same age."

"Did I talk that much?"

"Possibly more." He chuckled when she pretended to be outraged. "I don't think Travis minds."

"That's good. Just let me know if he ever says anything about it, and I'll talk to her."

"Katie keeps him from being lonely. He used to ask when he was going to have a baby brother or sister."

"Do you mind me asking why you didn't have another baby?"

"I wanted another, but she didn't."

Katie came over to the car with their Cokes and handed them through the window but didn't get in. "Some kids from Trav's school and mine are over there at the picnic tables. Can we hang out with them for a little while?"

Since they could see the group of kids from the car, she pushed aside her moment of motherly worry. "That's fine, Katie Cat. Just stay in that area with the tables where I can see you."

"Okay, Mommy." In her usual style, she skipped back to Travis and the other kids.

"Yep, just like her mommy." He slid his arm from the seat back to rest around her, his hand massaging her shoulder.

His touch was stirring up tingly sensations low in her belly. "She is growing up so fast." She rolled up the window and behind the tinted glass, they could see the kids, but it would be hard for anyone to see them. There was a moment of quiet, and the vibration of sexual tension in the air was almost palpable.

"Did you come to the drive-in a lot before it closed?" she asked.

"Most weekends. It was a popular hangout spot when I was in high school. It closed at the beginning of my senior year."

"So, you were old enough to make out in your car. I was still in middle school."

He chuckled. "Do you think I did a lot of making out in cars?"

She rubbed her cheeks, suddenly warm from blushing. Thankfully they were in the dark. "Highly likely. You were really popular in high school."

"Do you regret not having the opportunity for make-out sessions at the drive-in movies?"

"I kind of do. I wish I'd had the chance to experience this place as an older teenager. Seems like a rite of passage that I missed out on."

His arm tightened around her, pulling her snug against his side and gazing down at her with a hint of a sexy grin tipping up one corner of his mouth. It was dark in the car, but there was enough light coming in the windshield to make his dark brown eyes shine.

He leaned forward and looked around her to where the kids were hanging out with their friends. "It's never too late. Just because you are a few years past being a teen, that doesn't mean you can't make out in a back seat. You're never too old to experience something for the first time."

Her breath stuttered and caught. "I'm suddenly feeling like a teenager." She licked her lips and felt powerful when he groaned and swayed toward her.

He pulled her in a little closer. "You are a beautiful, smart, sexy woman."

In his fun-loving and teasing way, he was giving her what she had missed out on. Her pulse was racing, her skin hot and flushed. Aching to feel the warmth of his skin, she brushed her fingertips across his cheek, smooth from a fresh shave. She knew what this long awaited and dreamed about moment meant to her. But what did it mean to him?

He put his hand over the top of hers and kissed the tips of her fingers and then the palm of her hand. An electric spark zipped through her, and she shivered.

His breath was warm against her lips. So close she could taste the mint from his candy.

"I really want to kiss you," he whispered.

Wasting no time on needless words, she grasped the front of his sweater and tipped her head enough that their lips brushed softly. What was intended to be only a brief kiss, a token of what this back seat experience was like, took on a life of its own, morphing into a deep and searching kiss. Pulling back after one taste would take more willpower than she currently possessed.

Her silly worry that the real thing wouldn't live up to her years of fantasizing about Liam was put to rest. Their kiss not only lived up to and exceeded her expectations, it was a new level of amazing. It took mammoth effort to end the kiss because each time one of them tried to, the other pulled them back in for more. If the kids weren't expected back at any moment, they would not have forced themselves to end their first make-out session in the back seat of a car.

When the movie started, the kids joined them, but under one of the blankets that Nicole always carried in the car, she and Liam held hands through the whole movie.

* * *

Nicole didn't set her alarm clock that night and let herself sleep past sunrise the next morning. Even so, she hadn't gotten much sleep. Thoughts of Liam had kept her awake and smiling late into the night, and she woke with a smile on her face and didn't feel tired. She was running on the pure endorphins produced by Liam's kisses. She had a leisurely Sunday morning breakfast with her family and then got dressed to go get some baking done. And to see the man who had reawakened her libido in a big way.

When Nicole got to Sip & Read, the closed bookstore was dark and quiet. She peeked into the office, but it was empty, so she went through to the kitchen and got started on a batch of tarts. A little while later, the squeak of the apartment door and Liam's voice drifted down the stairwell. He came racing down with his cell phone pressed to his ear and talking rapidly.

He smiled at her and put his hand over the phone. "I forgot about a virtual meeting I have with an author. I'll be in my office." He left the kitchen before she could say a word.

Nicole told herself not to be disappointed because that was just silly. He wasn't avoiding her on purpose. He was just busy, and they were both adults who had jobs and lives to live. But still, she was so preoccupied that she almost burned the batch of tarts, which was something she never did.

When Travis came into the kitchen, he was dressed in dark jeans and a button-up shirt. "Morning."

"Good morning. What are your plans for the day?"

"As soon as Dad is done with his meeting on the computer, we are going to take Abuela to see her friend near Austin. I'm going because her grandson is a friend of mine."

"That sounds fun."

"Sorry I can't help you bake today."

"No problem." She swallowed back more disappointment. It didn't look like she would get to spend any time with Liam today. Before either of them could say more, Liam pushed through the swinging door.

"Sorry my meeting took so long. Are you ready to go?" he asked his son.

"Yep. Ready."

Liam smiled at her once again. "I'm not sure what time we will be back. Will you make sure everything is locked up before you go home later?"

"Of course." There was a hesitation and because Travis was with them, they could not repeat their kiss from the night before or discuss what had happened between them.

"Dad, we're late."

"I know. Let's go."

"You two have fun today," she said as they rushed out the door.

An uncomfortable knot started to form in her

YOU pick your books – WE pay for everything.
You get up to FOUR New Books and TWO Mystery Gifts...absolutely FREE!

Dear Reader,

I am writing to announce the launch of a huge **FREE BOOKS GIVEAWAY**... and to let you know that YOU are entitled to choose up to FOUR fantastic books that WE pay for.

Try **Harlequin® Special Edition** books featuring comfort and strength in the support of loved ones and enjoying the journey no matter what life throws your way.

Try **Harlequin® Heartwarming™ Larger-Print** books featuring uplifting stories where the bonds of friendship, family and community unite.

Or TRY BOTH!

In return, we ask just one favor: Would you please participate in our brief Reader Survey? We'd love to hear from you.

This FREE BOOKS GIVEAWAY means that your introductory shipment is completely free, <u>even the shipping</u>! If you decide to continue, you can look forward to curated monthly shipments of brand-new books from your selected series, always at a discount off the cover price! <u>Plus you can cancel any time</u>. Who could pass up a deal like that?

Sincerely

Pam Powers

Pam Powers
For Harlequin Reader Service

Complete the survey below and return it today to receive up to 4 FREE BOOKS and FREE GIFTS guaranteed!

FREE BOOKS GIVEAWAY
Reader Survey

1	**2**	**3**
Do you prefer stories with happy endings?	Do you share your favorite books with friends?	Do you often choose to read instead of watching TV?
◯ YES ◯ NO	◯ YES ◯ NO	◯ YES ◯ NO

YES! Please send me my Free Rewards, consisting of **2 Free Books from each series I select** and **Free Mystery Gifts**. I understand that I am under no obligation to buy anything, no purchase necessary see terms and conditions for details.

❑ **Harlequin® Special Edition** (235/335 HDL GRM5)
❑ **Harlequin® Heartwarming™ Larger-Print** (161/361 HDL GRM5)
❑ **Try Both** (235/335 & 161/361 HDL GRNH)

FIRST NAME   LAST NAME

ADDRESS

APT.#   CITY

STATE/PROV.   ZIP/POSTAL CODE

EMAIL ❑ Please check this box if you would like to receive newsletters and promotional emails from Harlequin Enterprises ULC and its affiliates. You can unsubscribe anytime.

Your Privacy – Your information is being collected by Harlequin Enterprises ULC, operating as Harlequin Reader Service. For a complete summary of the information we collect, how we use this information and to whom it is disclosed, please visit our privacy notice located at https://corporate.harlequin.com/privacy-notice. From time to time we may also exchange your personal information with reputable third parties. If you wish to opt out of this sharing of your personal information, please visit www.readerservice.com/consumerschoice or call 1-800-873-8635. **Notice to California Residents** – Under California law, you have specific rights to control and access your data. For more information on these rights and how to exercise them, visit https://corporate.harlequin.com/california-privacy.

SE/HW-122-FBG22_SE/HW-122-FBGVR

belly. She was bummed that he wouldn't be around today and also a little worried that he might be regretting what had happened between them in the back scat at the drive-in.

Chapter Eleven

From the moment Nicole opened her front door, the savory scent of her mom's Swedish meatballs made her mouth water. "It smells delicious in here."

"Hi, honey. Did you get a lot of baking done today?"

"Yes, I did." Mimi looked adorable with the new short and sassy haircut that Katie had talked her into. She'd even colored her gray back to her dark brown.

"Everyone I talk to around town has been raving about your baking."

Feeling suddenly taller, she let herself soak in the compliment. Knowing that her hometown folks were enjoying her cooking was another goal accomplished. "That's always nice to hear." Because she had forgotten to plug her phone in last night, it had died so she plugged it in with the charger on the kitchen counter.

"Katie is already over at Jenny's. They stopped by earlier and picked her up. Lilly was too excited to wait because she wanted to show Katie the new furniture her daddy made for her playhouse."

"She has the most wonderful playhouse I've ever seen." It was a miniature version of Barton Estate, the big historic home that Eric had restored with the intent of selling. When Jenny became their nanny, it hadn't taken long for them to realize they belonged together, and they made the old house their home. "Did she pack a bag for her sleepover with Lilly?"

"Yes. I checked and made sure she had everything she needs."

"Give me a few minutes to check my email and then change clothes, and I'll be ready to go over to Jenny's house."

"The meatballs need about ten more minutes, and then I have to transfer them into the travel dish. No rush."

At the kitchen table, she opened her laptop and then her email account. Junk mail went straight into the trash, and a few other messages that didn't need immediate attention could wait until tomorrow. She continued scrolling until one caught her eye.

Smokey Mountain Resorts.

The sudden spike of excitement made her heart beat so hard she could feel it in her throat and grew momentarily light-headed. She shook out her hands in preparation to open the email.

Was this her chance to get back into the culinary game with the big leagues?

Instead of opening it right away, she closed her eyes and took a moment. This resort wasn't her top choice, but it was her second and it was a really good job that would come with great pay and benefits, like medical insurance. With a few deep breaths and a silent prayer, she opened the email.

Thank you for applying to Smokey Mountain Resorts. We were impressed by your résumé. However, at this time, our head chef has decided to stay on with us.

Her spike of adrenaline spiraled down into the pit of her stomach where it curdled like vinegar in milk. Today's mood, which was already shaky because she wasn't sure where she stood with Liam, took a crash and burn nosedive straight into the garbage.

Once she knew she wouldn't throw up, she made herself read the rest of the email.

The only positions we have open are for jobs way below your skill level. We will certainly keep you in mind for future openings.

Even though she had a strong urge to slam close her laptop, she did it slowly and dropped her head into her hands.

"What's wrong, honey," her mother said from behind her.

"I heard back from one of my job applications, and it's not good news."

"I'm sorry."

"That's one more shot at a career knocked off my list." All she could hear was Jeff's voice repeating the same phrase. *You wasted that money on culinary school.* A burst of hot pain burned in the back of her throat.

"I know this is not the news you hoped for, but when it is meant to be it will happen. When it's right, you'll know it." Mimi opened the lid on the skillet and checked the meatballs.

The chair legs scraped against the floor as she stood with more force than she'd intended. "There is only one left to hear from. I guess I need to start putting in more applications."

"You know you are welcome to live here for as long as you want. In fact, I'm okay with you never leaving, and I know Liam likes having you work with him."

I work for *him, not* with *him.*

She paced from the table to the refrigerator and back again. Having ownership of her own place would be a different story, but without a high-paying job, there was zero chance of that.

"Maybe you should truly consider staying in Oak

Hollow because I know everyone in town would like to have you continue cooking and baking for them."

"But I spent so much money on culinary school. I have to have a career that makes it worth spending that much money."

Her mom stroked her head like she had done when she was a little girl. "I know you are disappointed, honey. But don't worry about money. You'll feel better once we get over to Jenny and Eric's for dinner."

Nicole shook her head. "I'm not fit company for anyone right now." She didn't even want to be around herself at the moment. "You go and give my regrets. I'm going to get in bed and not get out until I figure out what to do next, and I don't know when that will be."

"Nicole, I hate to see you like this. I know how you can get down on yourself. Come be around family and let us cheer you up."

"I really need time alone to process and adjust my plans and expectations. I don't want to answer the phone or the door. I just want to get into bed, and since Katie is spending the night with Lilly, I won't have to worry about her seeing me bummed out like this."

"Are you sure?"

With tears stinging her eyes, she was more than sure. "Please, Mom. I never get time completely alone. I need this. Just me in a house with no one else in it."

"Okay. I can understand that. I remember being a busy mom with young kids. You call me if you change your mind and don't want to be alone or just want someone to listen."

"Thanks, Mom. I'll see you tomorrow." She kissed her cheek and then started up the stairs, each step harder and harder. She just needed a few hours to work through this setback and get on the right track.

Safely behind the bathroom door, she let her shoulders sag on a long groan. She knew she was acting like a whiny baby, but she couldn't help it. She got into the shower, leaned her forehead against the new marble tiles and allowed the first tears to fall. She rarely cried, but when she did, it was only when no one was around to see or hear her. She'd been judged or shamed too many times by her husband to cry in front of people. She knew perfectly well that her mom wouldn't shame her, but the last ten years had programmed her to hide her emotions.

She'd learned to act as if everything was fine and dandy, even when it wasn't. She'd learned that from the master of fooling people. For the last five years, she and Jeff had basically been living as roommates, but no one knew that but them. Because he had never been violent and was absent from their daily lives more often than not, she'd made the best of their situation.

Once she was dry and in her pajamas, she burrowed under her comforter. If only her brain would just shut off so she could sleep, but it wouldn't. Like always, she'd have to think through everything one step at a time before she could make a good plan.

The Smoky Mountain Resort would've been a good job. A really good job. But her number one choice with Hamilton Resorts was still a possibility. All hope wasn't lost, but she still really needed this time alone. She'd let someone try to cheer her up tomorrow.

Over the last few months, and years, she'd had to be so strong for Katie. Her daughter deserved at least one parent who was there for her 100 percent. Through everything they'd been through—an absentee husband and father, Jeff's bad moods, accident, funeral and then losing the only home Katie had ever known—she hadn't been able to hide herself away to grieve, cry and yell about her situation. Instead, she'd gathered up all the tiny broken pieces and packed them away in her mind in a little box labeled *The remains of a former life.*

Something about this most recent job rejection was striking her harder than it should—like the last straw pulled out that made everything topple. Probably because she was worried about where she stood with Liam.

Now was her chance to get in a good cry while no one was around.

Liam drove up to Winslet Farm and spotted Mimi backing her car out of the detached garage. She rolled down her window.

"Hello, Liam. Did Nicole call you?" Her normally cheery smile had been replaced with a furrowed brow.

"No. I was next door dropping off my mom." A bad sensation was creeping into his whole body. "You look worried. What's wrong?"

"Well…" Mimi worried her hands together while glancing at the upstairs window. "Nicole heard from one of the resorts, and she is really upset about not getting the job."

"Oh, no." He said the words, but a wave of relief came along with a touch of guilt. He was secretly happy because it meant she would be staying longer. Their kiss at the drive-in gave him hope that maybe they could eventually become more than friends. This would give him more time to convince her that this was where she needed to be.

Time for him to know if she would be leaving Oak Hollow. And him. He could not open himself up completely if she wasn't staying.

"Is she in the house?" he asked.

"Yes. She's been through so much lately and is so hard on herself. I understand wanting to do your best, but I don't know where she got this idea that she has to be perfect at everything and accomplish such lofty goals."

Liam had a hunch that it had something to do with her husband playing on her already strong drive and amplifying it to an unhealthy level. "What is she doing now?"

"She's taken to her room."

"She won't come out of her room?"

"She's done this since she was little. Just hides herself away until she thinks something through or works out a problem. Katie is over at Jenny and Eric's, and we were both supposed to go over for dinner, but she wants to stay home alone. She wants the house to herself and to hide away for a while."

"Think she'll talk to me?"

"I wish she would but probably not. She said she is not coming out of her room until tomorrow. She wants to be left alone."

"I have an idea. You should go have dinner with the family, and if you don't mind, I'm going to stay here for a while."

She patted his forearm. "Okay, honey. The door is locked, so just don't be upset if she won't let you in or take your call until morning."

"I won't."

Once Mimi had driven away, he headed for the front door but stopped after a few steps. She wasn't going to answer his knock, and rather than calling and getting her voice mail he grabbed hold of the lowest branch of the oak tree beside her bedroom window and hoisted himself up. It was a good thing he had on tennis shoes because if he had on his boots, he'd probably slip and fall out of the tree. Then he would be the one needing help. When he made it to the big branch that arched across the center of her window, he could see her curled up under a blanket, facing the other way, her dark curls spread across the pillow. Hooking one arm around a branch above him, he knocked on her window.

She shot into a sitting position and spun around to look at him with wide eyes. "Liam? What in the world are you doing? You're going to hurt yourself."

"Then open the window and let me in before I fall out of this tree."

She pushed aside the covers, revealing a pair of red-and-white flannel pajama bottoms and a dark green tank top. She looked like a lost Christmas present that he wanted to unwrap, but that's not what this tree-climbing mission was about.

It took a bit of effort for her to get the old wooden window to slide open but then she stood there with her hands on her hips, blocking his way into her room. She was trying to look fierce, but her eyes were red from crying. With her chest thrust forward—and no bra on—he was having a hard time focusing. She had awakened some part of him that had apparently been sleeping for forty-one years. She'd been right under his nose his whole life. What had taken him so long? How had he not seen her as this amazing woman until now?

"Liam Mendez, what are you doing in the tree outside my bedroom window?"

"I came to cheer you up. And I seem to recall

you saying you'd let me in if I climbed up to your window."

"I guess I did say that." Her lips trembled as if she was fighting a smile, and she stepped back.

One leg at a time, he climbed through the open window feetfirst. "I'm not letting you get down on yourself because of one missed job opportunity."

Nicole turned from the window, sat on the edge of her bed and covered her face with both hands. "It's not just this one job. It's…" She dropped her hands to her lap and cocked her head. "Wait. How'd you know that I needed cheering up?"

He sat on the twin bed across from hers, and with his legs stretched, his big feet where next to her petite ones. "While I was in the tree, a little bird told me."

"Very funny. I assume this little bird answers to the name Mimi?"

"Talk to me, Nic."

She flopped back onto the bed with her feet still on the floor and stared up at the ceiling where a few glow-in-the-dark stars remained from her teenage years. "What's to say? I didn't get the job at the Smokey Mountain Resort. End of story."

"I suspect there is more to this than just that."

She sighed. "I was in line for a promotion to head pastry chef at the resort where I was working in Montana, and I thought it was mine. But in a twist of the knife, the owner's whiny son was promoted to the position."

"Sounds like favoritism."

"After that, he looked for every reason to get rid of me because he knew I was a better chef than him and people were starting to notice. He's probably the reason I haven't gotten another job. Who knows what he is saying to people when they call for a reference?"

"That's not legal."

"I don't really believe that. I'm just telling myself stories to try and make myself feel better." She put her bare feet on top of his running shoes.

Her toenails were painted with a glittery red that made her look even more like a Christmas present that had been waiting just for him. "I can tell you have something more eating at you. Something you don't want to tell anyone. But you might feel better if you get it off your chest."

"Maybe."

"What better person to tell than the man who can keep the secret about the identity of the most secretive author around."

That got a pained laugh from her. "I don't want you to pity me or think less of me."

"Nic, that is not going to happen."

"You don't know that for sure."

"You said you'd let me in your window because

you trust me. So, trust me now. Trust me to listen and understand."

She looked at her lap and rubbed her thighs. "Trust is something that has become difficult for me."

He moved to sit beside her like he'd done while they were editing, because sometimes it was easier to talk about painful things when someone wasn't staring straight at you. "Because of Jeff?"

"Yes." She lay back on the bed with her legs across his lap. "I acted like everything was fine in front of other people. I got really good at performing and playing the happy wife over the years."

Because he'd been in the right—or wrong— place, he'd secretly witnessed one of their interactions and seen through her act. He took one of her tiny feet in both hands and worked his thumbs into her arch, making her toes flex. Her soft sigh told him she was starting to relax.

"Coming home to Oak Hollow wasn't a choice for me. It was desperation because I ran out of choices. I lost my job completely a few days after Christmas. And I lost—" Her voice broke, and she cleared her throat.

"Your husband."

She rubbed her cheeks and then picked at lint on her flannel pants. "I lost Jeff years ago."

"How do you mean?"

"We lived like roommates for years. We slept in rooms on opposite ends of the house. He was leading his life, and Katie and I were living ours. Separately."

Anger flared hot in his chest. Her jackass of a husband had not taken care of his family. He gritted his teeth and asked a question he dreaded the answer to. "Did he hurt you?"

"Never physically."

But the man *had* hurt her. She was wounded. That was clear in her demeanor and posture.

"When we first grew apart, I agonized over what he was out doing when he wasn't at home or at work. Then one day, I realized I didn't care what he was doing. But I should have paid more attention because he was out gambling away all of our money and our house."

"For real?"

"Unfortunately, yes."

"After his death, I looked into selling the house that we owned free and clear. It was one he inherited from his parents, but I learned that he had gambled it away right before he died. We were left with no home. He lost the only one Katie had ever known."

He clenched his jaw so tight that it hurt. "He was controlling, and he was not who he made people believe he was," Liam said.

She tipped her head and studied his face. "That's true. How did you know?"

It had only taken Liam one overheard conversation to figure out that her husband wasn't the guy he led people to believe. He hated thinking ill of the dead, but the man had been an ass. "A few years back, I overheard a conversation between you and Jeff."

"Really? When?"

He shifted to lay beside her and propped up on one elbow. "It was around Thanksgiving. I was down at the river and the two of you walked into the back of the pecan orchard. I did not like the way he was talking to you, but I stayed hidden, waiting to see if you needed me to intervene. I worried that if he knew I had overheard that he would take it out on you. I wasn't sure what he would do if he knew I was there, but now I wish I had done something."

"I'm afraid to know what you overheard."

Liam replayed what he remembered. He needed to choose his words carefully. *You need to let me handle it. I'm the one who makes the decisions.* Jeff hadn't been touching Nicole, but he had been leaning toward her in an intimidating manner. *You don't speak for me. Take care of our child and I'll handle the rest.*

When Nicole had tried to speak, he had shushed her. Liam wished now that he had said or done something, but he hadn't known the whole story about their relationship. He and Nicole hadn't been close enough friends in recent years for him to ask.

Liam lay on his back and looked up at the ceiling fan. "He was saying it was your job to take care of your child and his job to handle everything else. It sounded like you had said something that he took as you trying to speak for him, and he did not like that."

She sighed and put her head on Liam's shoulder, and he wrapped an arm around her. "I remember that conversation."

"I'm sorry, Nic. I don't mean to make you relive it."

"It's okay. Now that I know what you already know, it's not like too much of it will surprise you." She tipped her head and stared up at him. "I do have to ask you not to tell anyone else the things I've told you. My mom is the only one who knows about losing the house, but she doesn't know anything about the living separately or him never being around."

"Are you sure she doesn't know any of that?" He had a feeling Mimi knew more than Nicole realized. She'd never said anything bad about Jeff in front of him, but she always had a kind word to say about everyone. Not for Jeff.

She sighed and then smoothed her hand back and forth across his chest. "No, but that's what I'm choosing to believe. I've never told anyone. Except you. When she came to visit, Jeff would move back into my room. Had to keep up appearances."

Liam was scared to hear what else she had been through over the years. "You never considered getting a divorce?"

Her sigh was long and drawn out, but not upset.

"Are you really going to talk me into telling you my last dark secret?"

"Only if you want to tell me."

"I did ask him for a divorce…and that's the last time I saw him alive. It was the same day Jeff died," she said in a voice that was a whisper.

"Oh, Nic." He held her tighter. "I'm so sorry. What was it that made you ask on that day?"

"It was after I read *Her New Life* that I found the courage and strength to ask for a divorce."

Liam's heart jolted behind his rib cage.

What he'd overheard that day in the orchard had stuck with him, tumbling around in his mind until the villain of his bestselling book had emerged. What would she think if she knew the ex-boyfriend in her favorite book was modeled after her husband?

Chapter Twelve

Nicole snuggled against Liam's warm chest, breathing in his clean herbal scent. She'd thought she wanted to be alone to sulk and whine about her life not going as planned, but having Liam beside her was the comfort she hadn't known she needed. She couldn't believe he had so easily gotten her to open up and tell him things she had never planned to tell another living soul. And instead of being mortified that someone knew, it felt good to share her burdens with another.

She was trusting him with her secrets.

It had definitely helped her to voice her troubles and worries aloud. No wonder people paid for therapy. She was looking at everything with a calmer mind. The position at Smokey Mountain resort was just one job in a place she wasn't that interested in living, so maybe it wasn't meant to be, and like her mom had said, she'd know when something was right.

"Thank you for listening to me. I do feel better."

"I'm here for you anytime."

"I'm glad you are good at keeping secrets." She felt him tense, but then he adjusted his position so that they were face-to-face.

"I'll keep your secrets, sweetheart."

That was the first time he'd ever called her sweetheart, and the term of endearment send a sparkly feeling dancing across her skin. She didn't want him to leave, but she knew he would have to. They were both parents with responsibilities.

"Where is Travis?"

"He's at the apartment. When we got back to town, I dropped him off first and then brought my mom home. I should text him and let him know why I'm not home yet." He pulled his phone from his back pocket and started a text message.

On his back with his phone held above him, it highlighted the length of his arms. Nicole admired the shape of the muscles in his forearms shifting as he messaged back and forth with his son.

"He's fine. I told him I'd be home in an hour or so and he said he is not a baby and not to rush home on his account. He's on the computer editing his photos and videos."

"He's already such a good photographer. I think he really will make a career of it."

"That's what I think, too. I'm trying to support him in whatever way I can, but I still haven't found anyone to help him with his photography."

"He has such drive." She frowned. "Reminds me a little of myself. You might want to tell him not to be too hard on himself like I am."

He reached across her to put his phone on the nightstand and then pressed a lingering kiss on her forehead before settling back beside her.

His warm, soft lips felt good against her skin. But she needed more. She needed his mouth on hers and his hands everywhere all at once. Cuddled on her twin bed, the slow burn of passion flared to full life, burning her up from the inside. If he didn't kiss her soon, she was going to—

His lips met hers in an urgent need to connect and taste and tease. Twining her fingers in his short hair, she deepened their kiss. He took the hint and did not disappoint. His tongue moved softly against hers, and as their breath mingled, she tumbled happily into the flash fire of desire.

They were both breathless by the time he eased his lips from hers. He brushed her hair back from her face, letting his fingers trail slowly through her damp hair. "This time, there is no one outside the car who might see us through the window."

"And hopefully no one else in the tree," she said with a giggle.

"Better not be." His chuckle was deep and rumbly and made her shiver.

They were alone. Just the two of them, completely alone. She traced the angles of his jaw, something she'd wanted to do for so long. Their tentative caresses became bolder, their kisses deeper and more searching.

For how long they weren't sure, they kissed and touched and whispered, learning what the other one liked. His hands were like magic on her bare skin. Caressing. Playing. And driving her wild. She was about to take the leap and unzip his pants when the front door opened then closed. They both went completely still.

"I'm home, Nicole," her mom called up from the base of the stairs. "Good night."

"Good night," she yelled back to her, and then they laughed quietly with their hands over their mouths.

"I wish I could stay here with you all night, but I have to get back to Travis."

"I know. There will be other days and nights. I hope."

"You can count on it. Do I have to climb back out the window like a teenager, or do I get to use the front door?"

His playful grin made her giggle again. "Since

your car is out front, I think she knows you are here, and you are safe to use the front door." She reluctantly untwined her body from his and let him get off the bed.

He shoved his phone back into his pocket and then leaned down to kiss her. "Sweet dreams. Sleep well, and I'll see you in the morning."

"I'll see you then." Before he could turn to go, she grasped his hand. "Thank you for listening."

"Anytime."

She walked him to the door and kissed him once more before watching him walk down the dark stairway.

On the last step he reared back and clasped a hand to his chest. "Mimi, you startled me."

"Sorry." She chuckled. "I'm glad to see she let you inside."

When Liam coughed into his fist before clearing his throat, Nicole almost laughed.

"I'm glad she did too. She's going to be okay. She's strong and smart."

"Yes, she is."

Nicole had people who believed in her, and it made her want to walk a little taller and smile with more confidence.

Nicole was mixing buttercream frosting when Liam came into the kitchen, and after glancing around to see if they were alone, he leaned in for a kiss. It was a quick, sweet kiss but one that made her lips tingle and lovely memories and new ideas dance in her head.

Ideas that had the potential to change her future plans.

She dipped a spoon into the frosting and held it out to him. "Taste test. I'm trying out a new recipe with a secret ingredient."

Instead of licking the spoon, he brushed it against her mouth and then kissed her, swirling his tongue across her lips, giving her a lovely full body shiver.

He sucked lightly on her bottom lip before ending the kiss. "Delicious."

She was tempted to sigh like an infatuated young girl rather than the thirty-seven-year-old woman that she was.

He swiped his tongue across the back of the spoon. "What is the secret ingredient?"

"You'll have to guess. What did you come in here for? Do you have an order to place?" she asked.

"Nope. No order. Just a question. On Saturday, I need to go to San Antonio for a writer's conference. I have to take story pitches for a couple of hours and meet with a few people. If you think Amy and the others can handle the kitchen for the day, I'm hoping you will come with me."

Her belly gave a little swoop as if she was on a roller coaster. "I'd love to go. We will just be gone for the day?"

"Yes. We'll have to leave really early, but that shouldn't be a struggle since you are used to baker's hours."

"I can definitely handle early." While they talked, she began frosting maple pecan cupcakes.

"It will probably be bedtime before we get home."

"I can do enough prep in the kitchen that it should be fine."

"I'll make sure I have enough people scheduled to work on Saturday, and I guess the kids can stay with their grandmothers."

"Or just run back and forth between both houses like we did. It's very handy to have our mothers living next door to one another."

"It sure is. I'm glad you're going with me." He put the spoon in the sink. "I'm headed to the bank, but I'll be back soon."

"See you later." As soon as he was out of the kitchen, she turned up the volume on the music and did a little dance with her arms in the air and her hips swaying. They would have a whole day away from work and all the eyes and ears of their small town where almost everyone knew both of their histories.

Asking her to put the bistro in the hands of other people meant he really wanted her to go with him. She would have gone no matter where he'd wanted to take her, but a writer's conference had the added benefit of helping her on her newest venture into the world of publishing. If she was going to do something, she was going to do it to the best of her ability.

Which was why she couldn't give up on her culinary career. But it wouldn't be as much fun to edit and collaborate with Liam from a distance. A little ache crept into her chest.

Don't think about that now.

She didn't want to ruin the good mood she had going. Liam was helping her to remember who she'd been while growing up next door to him. The carefree girl who laughed and smiled and played. It was time to let some of her old self wake up. Time to have some fun and allow herself to feel some of the things she'd buried under years of pretending to the world that her marriage was okay even though it definitely wasn't.

Moving forward, caution was a must. She could not let herself get too deeply involved.

Or can I?

Kissing Liam Mendez, her fantasy man, was off the charts fantastic. She was letting herself feel again, and that was something she desperately needed.

There had been no conversation about the future, but they were both adults who knew that she wasn't going to be in Oak Hollow forever. But she'd be back to visit. Her family was here. Liam was here. She'd been very clear from the beginning that this was a temporary layover. Now, she just needed to keep reminding herself of that fact. She could not have a professional culinary career if she stayed here in small-town Texas.

Jeff's accusation that she'd wasted money on culinary school had put a fire under her already strong drive to have a successful career. She could not give up and let him be right.

All week, they stole kisses when no one was looking and squeezed in a few make-out sessions in his office or on the rooftop during their lunch break. By unsaid mutual agreement, they stayed away from his bedroom or hers because they both knew what would happen if they got that close to a bed. After almost going too far too fast in her bedroom that night he climbed the tree, they had kept their affections to kissing. It was so good between them, she wanted to enjoy the slow burn and excitement of discovering one another after so many years of knowing each other. It was fun, flirty and sexy. If her mom hadn't come home when she did that night, they might have ended up naked, but she was glad they hadn't…yet.

There was something to be said for a slow burn, like the couple in her favorite book, *Her New Life*.

Chapter Thirteen

Saturday morning, Nicole had her hair and makeup done and was dressed in navy blue slacks and a white sweater twin set. They were clothes comfortable for traveling but also professional enough to attend a conference. With a selection of car trip snacks and a thermos of coffee, she was ready ten minutes before Liam was scheduled to pick her up.

When he pulled into the driveway, it was still dark outside. The last of the silvery moonlight frosted the bare branches in the peach and pecan orchards. It would soon turn to golden light as the sunrise crested the horizon across the river. The air was still but damp enough to bite at her cheeks as she rushed for his black truck. Cold enough that she had made sure she had a coat this time.

The cab of his truck was warm and smelled deliciously of him. A mixture of herbal soap and a subtle cologne that reminded her of a walk in the woods after a spring rain. Would she still be here in the spring to walk in the rain and pick peaches? She would of course always come back for a visit, but with a new job, how often could she feasibly get away? She pushed away that concern for now. This day was too good to taint with worrisome thoughts.

"Good morning," she said. When he leaned her way across the console, she met him halfway for a kiss. He was more dressed up than she usually saw him. Gorgeous as ever in a pearly gray button-up and black slacks.

He pressed his lips once more to hers in a lingering caress that made her sigh. "Kissing you is a nice way to start the day."

His deep voice in the dark cab of the truck made her think of the drive-in movie. "It certainly is." She hoped to have the chance to wake up beside him and kiss him throughout the night at some point soon.

"Did you remember to bring a notebook so you can take notes when you are in some of the classes and workshops?"

She patted the bag at her feet as he turned the car around. "I have two notebooks, a variety of pens and…" She pulled out a divided container with a lid. "Road trip snacks." She didn't mention the emergency beauty supplies like makeup and a hairbrush that she had tucked away in the bottom of her bag. He didn't need to know she was so concerned about always looking her best around him.

"You get another A-plus as a travel companion."

"Is that the only reason you invited me?"

"No, it's just an added perk." He turned around in the circular gravel driveway in front of the house. "What did you bring?"

"A croissant with ham and cheese for you, mini muffins and the doughnut holes that you liked so much."

"My mouth is watering."

Her phone made the wind chime sound she'd programmed for email alerts, and she jerked it out of her purse's side pocket.

"Checking for news about job applications?" he asked.

His voice sounded irritated, and she glanced his way, wondering about his reaction. "Not specifically." She had a feeling he didn't want her to get another job, but was it because he wanted her to keep running the bistro or because he wanted *her* to stay in Oak Hollow?

Her heart squeezed when she saw the email.

It was the long-awaited final report from the investigation into Jeff's death. Hopefully, she'd finally have answers to whether or not asking him for a divorce might have distracted or upset him enough to get careless and cause the accident that took his life. Her guilt would either be put to rest or…

She stopped hesitating and opened the email. The wealth of tension and guilt she'd been carrying like a weight around her neck started to ease. It was officially ruled as an accident due to equipment failure that Jeff had no control over. Even if he had been distracted, that had not played a part in the accident. She had not had a hand in causing her husband's death. Relief mixed with grief and hit her in a sudden wave of emotion. She covered her mouth to hold back a choked sob.

"Is everything okay?" Liam slowed, pulled onto the side of the farm road and put the truck in Park.

"Yes. It's okay." She shifted in her seat to see him better. "The email is not about a job. It's about Jeff's accident at the lumber mill."

"What does it say?"

"The investigation revealed that he was not at fault. It was a senseless accident that he had no control over."

"They thought otherwise?"

"There was some question about it." She dropped her phone into her lap and clasped her hands to her cheeks. "Thank God it wasn't my fault."

"How could it have been yours?"

"Because it happened only a few hours after I asked him for a divorce. I've been afraid that he was upset or distracted and that led to his death."

"Oh, sweetheart." He opened his arms and leaned forward enough to hug her across the console, stroking her hair and kissing her forehead. "Have you been blaming yourself all these months?"

"A little bit," she said into the warmth of his neck.

He eased away from her and cradled her face before placing one tender kiss on her lips. "I'm glad it's been cleared up."

"Me, too. It's a huge weight lifted from my mind. Like a fog is clearing. I want to cry and laugh at the same time."

"Do it," he said. "I'll turn the music up loud and you can scream."

She chuckled. "Maybe later. Don't be surprised if I do it at some point when you least expect it." Needing to get her mind on other things, she opened the container of food and offered it to Liam.

"Thanks." He took the croissant and bit into it. "Mmm. So good."

She chose a mini banana nut muffin and chewed slowly. "Selfishly, I'm relieved by the official report, but Jeff is still gone, forever. And even though he often made me feel bad, I hate thinking that in his last moments he was upset."

"That's because you are a good person with a big heart. Is there anything else you have to do? What happens next?"

"Now, I will get the insurance money."

If only she'd had the money sooner, maybe she

could have saved her house, but then again, if she'd done that, she wouldn't be here. She wouldn't be sitting in a truck on the side of the road with Liam Mendez. And she wouldn't be…this happy. She wasn't lonely anymore.

Once they got back on the road, the two-hour trip went by quickly. The convention hall in San Antonio was huge and bustling with people and a buzz of excited activity. The air was just warm enough to be comfortable and scented with a faint fragrance that she knew from experience was added for a calming effect. Clusters of excited writers, mostly women, were sharing hugs and catching up. Laughter and excited waves bounced across the large open space.

They signed in and got their badges and a schedule for the day's classes and events like book signings and publisher talks. They'd only been there a few minutes and at least ten people had already said hello to Liam. But she couldn't help noticing that he seemed a little jumpy, glancing around like there was someone or something he needed to avoid. What did he have to be nervous about? This was his world.

But…he had left most of his old city life behind. Could there be more to why that happened than he'd told her?

They made their way into a ballroom where she looked over the class options and circled the ones that interested her the most before listening to a morning keynote speaker. The bestselling romance author gave a very motivational talk and some advice about not giving up, which resonated with Nicole.

Liam took hold of her hand as they made their way through the crowd and back out into the wide hallway that led to all the breakout session rooms. It was time for him to listen to optimistic authors pitch their story ideas in an attempt to get their books published.

"I need to get to my first meeting," he said. "Are you sure you don't want to come and pitch your story?"

"I don't feel ready for that, yet. I need to make my story better first."

"Okay. I'll meet up with you for lunch." He didn't kiss her but squeezed her hand with a smile meant only for her.

She stood there and watched him walk away. He was such a striking figure. She was tempted to yell out for everyone to hear that he was here with her. He was spoken for.

Liam walked into his assigned room where six small tables, each with two chairs, were spaced out across the brightly colored carpeting. Rebecca, who was his editor—although no one knew that but her and a handful of others—waved from across the room. She had on her usual colorful cat's-eye glasses, layers of beaded necklaces lay against her silky black dress and today her hair had a few turquoise streaks running through her silver bob. She had been in the publishing business for thirty-five years and taught him more than anyone else along the way to where he was now.

She met him halfway and gave him an enthusiastic hug that was surprisingly strong for such a petite woman whose head only came up to the center of his chest. "We miss having you in the office. No one else has your knack for keeping us on track during a meeting or can make me laugh like you."

"I miss you, too. Tell me about what's been going on."

"I have a new editorial assistant, and she is fabulous. Thank goodness she is willing to help me handle my social media accounts. Are you still laying low on social media?"

"Yes. I am staying completely away from it. I don't know that I will ever go back. I just don't see the need for it."

"You know, all the talk has died down." She glanced around and lowered her voice. "I think everyone has completely forgotten about that…person who took your words completely out of context and twisted them into something of a complete fabrication. Talk about fiction writing…" She rolled her eyes and flicked a hand loaded with jeweled rings.

He couldn't hold in a chuckle. He'd missed Rebecca's dramatic personality and dry humor. "Too bad she didn't use a good editor. She certainly didn't use a fact checker."

"It is probably safe for you to come back to the world of online interaction. Maybe just dip your toe back in with one account."

"I don't think so." The whole smear campaign had been a pointless mess. Cheap entertainment for people who didn't care about the truth so much as the shock value and number of likes and comments.

"Ladies and gentlemen," said a man in the center of the room. "The doors will open in a few minutes and the first authors will begin coming inside. You will have five minutes with each author before a bell will sound and they will move on to the next table. I hope you find some amazing stories and talent."

Liam and Rebecca made their way toward their tables, which happened to be next to one another. "Are you looking for any specific types of stories today?"

"I'm hoping for a good paranormal with a new twist or something with musicians."

"I'm looking for a rom-com with witches and maybe a good cozy mystery. But you know what I'm hoping for most." She winked at him.

He knew she was talking about another book from him, and he had yet to tell her he was working on it. "You just might get your wish."

Her blue eyes lit up and she clapped her hands rapidly in front of her chest. "You have just made my day. We have got to find time to talk in private very soon."

As he took his seat, two women he didn't know at the opposite corner of the room were glancing his way as they talked in hushed tones. He couldn't hear what they were saying, and it most likely had nothing to do with him, but he still got a knot in the pit of his stomach. As introverted as he was, he had always hated being the center of attention, and after the contrived and malicious social media fiasco, he loathed it.

Guarding his privacy had become very important to him.

While Liam did his editor thing and had a few other meetings, Nicole went to three workshops and took tons of notes, grabbing handouts whenever they were available. She learned about writing snappy dialogue, plotting a book and writing sex scenes—which gave her a few ideas she like to try out in real life. Too bad Liam wasn't in this workshop with her. But then again, if he had been, she would have blushed from the roots of her hair to the tips of her toes. When the class was over, she got up to leave and saw him standing in the back of the room. He smiled at her across the sea of people, and her heart fluttered.

"Talk about tall, dark and handsome," a woman beside her said to a friend. They were looking right at Liam. "Is he one of the book cover models?"

"He must be," the second woman said. "I'd like to write a sex scene with him as my inspiration."

"Me, too." Nicole couldn't resist joining their conversation. "He's actually not a cover model. He is an editor."

"No kidding?"

As he drew close and it was obvious that he was heading their way, they looked between him and Nicole.

"He's a friend," she said to them.

"You go girl," one of them said as Nicole left them to meet Liam in the middle of the room.

"How were your meetings?" she asked him.

"Good. I heard a few story ideas that hold a lot of promise and got to catch up with a few old friends. Did you learn anything?"

"I sure did. And I got a few good ideas."

"Let's go eat. I'm starving."

She chuckled and hooked her arm through his. "That's nothing new."

Being around all of the book talk and so many professional writers increased her excitement to continue working on her manuscript. She had jotted down ideas for her story and couldn't wait to get her fingers on the keyboard once they got home.

At lunch, he introduced her to so many people

she couldn't keep all the names straight. They went to a book signing for his publishing house and then together they attended one more workshop about doing research for your book.

Nicole was exhausted from all the excitement but having a fabulous time. "Thank you for inviting me to come along with you today."

"I'm glad Katie let your secret out of the bag, or I wouldn't have known you were interested in writing."

"So am I. Sometimes her constant chatter can be a good thing."

"Are you ready to get out of here and head for home?" he asked.

"Yes. You can tell me about everything on the drive, and I can share some new ideas for my book."

They had been inside the convention hall all day and not paying attention to the world going on outside, so it was a surprise when they walked out the doors and were hit with a blast of icy wind. She gasped and clutched her arms around herself. The sharp bite of cold made him utter a few choice words. They had left their coats in the truck so they wouldn't have to carry them around all day, but that suddenly seemed like a mistake.

"I thought the cold front wasn't supposed to come in until tomorrow morning."

He shivered and took hold of her hand. "This is my fault. I should have kept a closer eye on the weather. Let's get to the truck." He took a step and his foot slipped to the side, and he almost went down but quickly caught his balance. "There is already ice forming."

She looked at the patches of ice and then up to the overhang above the doors. "I think it's just from water dripping off the edge of the roof. Hopefully the roads aren't icy."

"Let's go back inside and make a plan."

Taking careful steps to avoid any more ice, they made it into the warmth of the convention hall. He pulled her shivering body against his and rubbed her back.

"We can't drive all the way back to Oak Hollow if there is any chance of ice on the roads," she said. "We have to cross too many bridges and elevated sections of highway."

"You're right. We have to stay here for the night."

Chapter Fourteen

Liam's heart was racing both from almost slipping and busting his butt on the ice, but more so because he would get to spend the whole night with Nicole. He felt bad about not paying more attention to the unpredictable Texas weather—known for changing from temperatures that allowed for shorts to needing coats in the span of a day. But this wasn't all bad news. The prospect of staying the night in a hotel room with Nicole was the best news he'd heard in a long time.

He pulled out his cell phone to check the weather and saw several missed calls. "My mom called. Four times."

"Oops. I have missed calls too," Nicole said.

Because they had been in workshops, they had

put their phones on silent, so they had both missed calls from their mothers. They found a somewhat quiet spot, and both called home.

The phone only rang once before his mom answered. "Mijo, are y'all okay?"

"Yes, we're fine. Sorry we had our phones on silent so we wouldn't interrupt any of the speakers."

"You're still at the conference and not on the roads?"

"We're still here. The weather has taken a turn."

"I know. That's why I've been calling and so has Nicole's mom."

"She is talking to her now." He smiled at Nicole who was using her free hand to animatedly emphasize whatever it was she was saying.

"You two will have to stay in San Antonio tonight. By the time you get closer to the Hill Country, everything will be getting icy. We already have sleet starting to stick. The roads simply aren't safe to travel on. Not safe at all."

Lidia Mendez tended to exaggerate when she felt it was called for, and he had a strong feeling she was up to something, like a bit of matchmaking, but this time he didn't mind. On her end of the line, a laugh very similar to Nicole's was followed by his son's voice. "Is that Katie I hear in the background?"

"Yes. We're next door at their house because Travis thought we needed to check on them."

It made him proud that his son was so thoughtful. "I'm glad you are all together and safe."

"We are listening to the weather on the battery-powered radio right now."

"Why the radio?"

"The electricity went out about an hour ago because of the wind that kicked up. I've already called the electric company, and they are working on it. It is currently still okay in San Antonio, but by the time you get halfway home, the roads won't be safe."

"I know, Mom. I won't put us in danger."

"We are toasty warm in front of the fireplace playing games and doing some indoor camping. You don't need to worry about your children, and we would like not to worry about ours, so promise me you will not try to drive."

"I promise." Since everyone was safe, he was glad for the reason to stay here with Nicole. Mother Nature had decided that their getaway from Oak Hollow should be extended, and he was on board with that plan. "I'll make sure to leave my phone on now, so call if you need to. I'm going to see about finding us a place to stay."

"Very good. Stay safe. Love you, Mijo."

"Love you, too." He hung up and smiled at Nicole who had already ended her call. "Did you get the whole story about them being at your house?"

"Yes. Katie is excited by the adventure of their

situation. They are sitting by the fireplace playing
games and eating ice cream."

"Ice cream in this weather?" Her laughter was
a melodic sound that took him back to the days of
playing at the river and running through the orchard
to pick a fresh peach. A tiny piece of the soundtrack
from his childhood. It was nice to hear Nicole laughing a little more each day.

"You are going to have to blame your son for that.
He said they should eat it because if the electricity
is out for too long, it will melt."

"Sounds like something I would've said as a kid."

"I think it's something you would say now." She
stepped close enough to put a hand on his chest.

"True." He wrapped her in his arms and shivered
when her delicate hands roamed up and down his
back. They were in public and touching in a way
lovers might, but no one here knew their situation.
No one here would talk or judge. "There is a hotel
connected to this convention center."

She kept her arms around his waist. "This conference is big, and most of the people I have talked
to are from out of town and are here for a couple of
days. What are the chances of there being an available room?"

"I don't know but let's find out." Hand in hand,
they followed a sign pointing them to the hotel.

"You're okay with sharing a room, right?"

"Absolutely." His skin grew warm, and he gave

her fingers a gentle squeeze, glad she'd brought it up first. "Hopefully we don't have to walk out into this weather to find something else."

"Or sleep in the lobby," she said as they neared a collection of black leather seating, none of which looked comfortable enough to sleep on.

"I won't let that happen."

He'd find somewhere for them to sleep. A comfortable place where they could be completely alone to continue exploring the desire between them. A place to relax without the chance of anyone walking into the room or needing their attention to check homework or track down a shipment of books. Their children were safe with their grandmothers, and they had the whole night to continue catching up and really learn who the other one had become. Over the last few weeks, he'd gotten a taste of what loving her might be like, but only enough to make him crave more.

The hotel's reception desk was polished white marble and topped with arrangements of fresh flowers. Classical music played at an almost imperceptible level but added a calming effect.

"Good evening," said an extremely tall young man in a suit and tie. "How can I help you?"

"Do you by any chance have available rooms for tonight?" Liam asked.

"You are in luck, my friend. I had a group of people check out a few hours ago to try and beat the unexpected early arrival of the winter storm, and I'm down to only one room left. Would you like the room?"

"We'll take it," she said.

He forced himself not to chuckle—or to give a whoop of happiness—about her eagerness to get the hotel room. He pulled out his wallet and credit card before Nicole could even get hers from her purse. But what should or should not happen between them tonight? If they took their developing relationship to a new level they'd yet to fully explore, what would that mean for their future? Would it change her mind about leaving Oak Hollow at her first opportunity or would it just leave him to pick up the pieces of his heart after she left?

Questioning her about her job search at faraway locations might seem too much like he was asking her to give up on her dreams. Nicole had to make up her own mind about what was best for her and her child. She had to decide how important their relationship was. How important he was.

With a key card in hand and no luggage, they found the elevator and rode in silence up to their floor, neither mentioning the fact that they were about to spend the night together in a hotel room. He'd forgotten to even ask if it had one or two beds. When the door swung open, there was a king-size bed covered with a crisp white comforter and gray pillows lined up across the front of a navy blue padded headboard.

He dropped the key card onto the dresser beside a TV. "Want to take a hot shower and warm up?"

Her lips parted in surprise, and whatever she'd been about to say was lost.

He hadn't meant that they should take a shower together, which appeared to be what she was thinking, but now that the idea was in his head... That was exactly what he wanted to do, but Nicole still looked shell-shocked and hadn't said a word. The last thing he wanted to do was take advantage of this situation or her.

"You get the shower first," he said, clearing up what he meant. "I'll go back down to the gift shop and buy toothbrushes and a few things we might need tonight."

She let out a slow breath. "Okay. Sounds good."

He rushed out the door and rolled his eyes at himself. He was a forty-one-year-old man and suddenly had the libido and composure of an eighteen-year-old. Now that he knew her marriage had been over for years, all kinds of ideas were popping up in his mind. A long list of experiences that he should have enjoyed years ago.

There was also a fear that kept replaying, fighting to be heard under the roar of his lust. He did not want to be her rebound guy. He'd had a rebound fling right after his divorce was finalized, and it had not gone well. If it went wrong between him and Nicole, it could not only leave one of them hurt—probably him when she left for a job—but it could ruin their lifelong friendship.

Once he located the gift shop, he bought toothbrushes, toothpaste, a Welcome to Texas sleep shirt for Nicole and a couple of things for himself, one of which was a just-in-case box of condoms. The water was running in the shower when he walked back into the room but as soon as it turned off, he knocked on the bathroom door.

"Nic, I bought you something to sleep in."

"Oh, thank you." The door opened a crack and floral scented steam curled out with one of her delicate hands.

He draped the shirt across her hand and then the door closed. If this was a romance novel, she would have flung open the door and pulled him inside with her. But this was real life. He couldn't remember ever being this nervous around a woman, but Nicole wasn't just any woman. He needed to know what she was thinking and where her head was because he couldn't mess this thing up. There was so much history between them, and their lives were forever intertwined. Now that he'd discovered the mature, beautiful woman she'd become, he could not risk losing their friendship.

When he got back home to his computer and the new book he'd started, he would be writing his own version of tonight's events. His book would now have a hotel scene, but in his version, the couple would shower together followed by no need for anything to sleep in.

He toed off his dress shoes and sat on the side of the bed to look over the room service menu. He could go for some food and drink. It would give them something to do while they figured out where tonight would take them.

The bathroom door swung open, and she emerged with wet hair, and the Welcome to Texas shirt hitting her above midthigh, exposing shapely legs that were quite different from the skinny girl he'd grown up with. He had always been a leg man, and hers were magnificent. They were toned and hinting at her doing something to keep in shape. She brushed her hands down the front of her shirt from waist to hem as if trying to make it longer. Was she completely bare beneath? He was hungry in a new kind of way.

She pointed to the words written across her chest. "This phrase is kind of perfect for me."

"Texas is happy you're home." He probably shouldn't have said the word *home*. Even though he hoped she would decide to stay and make Oak Hollow her home once again, he did not what to appear as if he was trying to influence her. Whatever she decided had to be her choice because he knew what could happen if someone was pushed to make a decision. He'd made that mistake with his wife.

He held up the menu. "Want to order some food? I'm hungry."

"That sounds great. Do they have anything that looks good?" She sat beside him, close enough to see the menu but not touching.

They decided what they wanted and while they waited for the order to arrive, he took a shower. When he came out of the bathroom wearing an orange-and-white-striped swimsuit, she was sitting up in bed with her back against the padded headboard, and the covers bunched around her waist.

Her dimples flashed, making her look younger. "Are you wearing a swimsuit?"

He shrugged. "It's the only thing I could find in my size."

A knock at the door had him changing directions. He tipped the waiter and then rolled the room service cart inside but took the tray of food off and put it on the middle of the bed. If she was uncovered and sitting at the table with her legs revealed, he'd be hard-pressed to resist tasting her along with the food and wine. He uncorked the bottle of red wine and poured two glasses before handing her one.

She pulled back the covers on his side of the bed. "Come on in. The water is fine."

He chuckled and slid between the cool sheets. This was the moment when his body laughed at his reasoning skills. Being in bed with her was going to be infinitely harder than sitting at the table. He'd been a fool to think otherwise.

"To riding out the storm in style," he said. Their glasses clinked with a musical chime.

"I'll drink to that. Mmm. You picked a good wine."

"Since we serve wine at Sip & Read, I've gotten more familiar with which ones are best."

She uncovered the food, and they split an order of pasta primavera and a BLT with cheese and then shared cheesecake for dessert.

He poured the last of the wine into their glasses, moved the tray of dishes back to the room service cart and pushed it into the hallway. He was happy to slip back into the warm bed beside her.

After one more sip of wine, she slid down in the bed to recline on her side and he mimicked her movement. Her cheeks were flushed a rosy shade of pink, something that always happened when she drank red wine. Her hair was drying into a full, lush tumble of curls, and something in her green eyes was calling to him in a way that made him wonder how he had possibly been blind to their connection his whole life.

"None of this food was anywhere close to as good as your cooking."

"You just want me to keep feeding you and your sweet tooth."

"I can't deny that, but that's because you do it so well. Culinary school was well worth whatever you paid for it."

Her eyes widened and so did her mouth before she smiled. "Wow. Thank you. That means…" She pressed her fingertips to her lips like she needed to contain some emotion. "That means so much more than you realize."

He knew she got plenty of compliments because he'd heard them firsthand. What was it about his statement that had made her have that reaction? "It's the truth. I suspect a lot of it is your natural talent, but your school taught you very well. You make me and my stomach very happy."

"Is it only my cooking?"

"No, sweetheart." He brushed his foot against hers. "Your cooking is only an extra perk. I'd want to be right here with you right now even if you couldn't boil water."

"Being around you makes me happy, too. I've missed you over the years, and you have reminded me of who I used to be back before… You know."

"I do." He slid his hand across the space between them and rubbed her arm, wishing she hadn't gone through such a hard time for so many years. If only he could have done something to help her sooner.

"Did you ever think we would find ourselves in a hotel room together like this? What are you grinning about?" he asked.

"Did I ever *think* it would happen or did I ever *wish* it would happen?" She bit one side of her lower lip, and then her teeth slipped free as she smiled. She crooked her finger and they moved close enough that their legs touched.

She is the sexiest woman I have ever seen.

His already heated body woke to a state he couldn't recall ever reaching. Holding himself back was growing next to impossible.

"Let's go with the wish."

Chapter Fifteen

The sexy rumble of Liam's voice both soothed and excited Nicole. If he only knew how much being around him was healing her. He reached for her hand, pressing their palms together as if comparing the size, and the sweetness of the gesture made her think that maybe he did know.

"You really want me to tell you about the wish I've had since I was a teenager?"

"More than anything." He laced his fingers with hers.

"Instead of just words, maybe I should show you instead." She trailed one finger on her free hand slowly up the inside of his arm from wrist to elbow. They were so close their legs were touching, and she couldn't wait to hold him skin to skin.

"You are quickly becoming one of the most amazing women I have ever known."

"Did you realize I had a crush on you when I was a teenager?"

"No, sadly I did not."

"I'm surprised you never picked up on it."

He shrugged. "Guess I wasn't the most perceptive teenage boy. When I left for college, you were just about to start high school."

"I know I was just a kid to you. Way too young for a college guy."

"Neither of us are kids now." He put his hand low on her thigh but held perfectly still. "When did this crush end?"

The wine had loosened her inhibitions, and her willpower to resist him was nonexistent at this point. "Who said it ever ended?"

His smile made his eyes crinkle at the corners. "I might be late to the party, but I can tell you that you are not in it alone, sweetheart."

Her whole body flooded with warmth and tingles in very specific places. "I like hearing that. Is there such a thing as a grown-up crush?"

"It gets the idea across, until we…" His hand slid farther up her thigh, leaving a trail of goose bumps, and there was a question and longing in his hesitation and eyes.

"Become lovers?" she asked.

A slow sexy smile took his face from handsome

to breathtakingly gorgeous. "Exactly what I was thinking. But only if you are—"

Before he could finish his sentence, she kissed him, slowly at first. Tenderly. Telling him with more than words that she wanted him. "I'm sure." With every touch of his bare skin against hers the desire built. Nicole had fantasized about a situation like this one so many times over the years, but never expected her wish to be granted. Yet here she was face-to-face with the guy who she had built up into her image of the ideal man.

His hand was warm on the bare skin of her leg, and his dark eyes holding her as sure as a hug. Holding her with tenderness and eagerness to learn everything about her.

Her shiver brought a surge of pleasure that promised great things. She liked him and he liked her. It was time to stop acting like the teenager she'd been when he first drew her attention in a way that was more than friends. Time to stop being afraid that she was going to upset someone or make a mistake or a wrong decision.

Why was she denying herself happiness for even one more second? She'd done that long enough, and it was time to go for what she wanted. "I used to fantasize about you sweeping me away to a hotel and making love to me all night long."

He slid his hand up farther still until his palm brushed softly over the bare skin of her hip and her back. He groaned and nuzzled his lips against her neck. "You are completely naked underneath that shirt."

"Yes, I am. Is my shirt in your way?"

"Yes!"

He said it so quickly that they both laughed. She lifted her arms, and he slid his hands under her shirt, slowly caressing her before pulling it over her head, leaving most of her body still covered by the sheet.

"And I think it's time that you went skinny dipping," she said, and slipped one finger beneath the waistband of his swimsuit.

"I hope we can always laugh together whether we are naked or clothed."

"I so agree with that." She loved that they could talk and laugh with one another even when they were about to make love for the first time. They were still them. Liam and Nicole. Their friendship was still there and had moved with them into the lovers they were becoming.

"Want to tell me more about what I did in this fantasy of yours?"

She shook her head. "First, I want you to do whatever comes naturally. And then I'll start telling you about some of my fantasies."

His sexy grin flashed and made her tingle everywhere. "Are there that many of them?"

"Yes, years and years of them. I was smarter than

you and figured out this thing between us way before you did."

"Sounds like I have a lot of catching up to do." He trailed his fingers across her collarbone and then down to lightly caress her breast in a move that was achingly erotic yet tender.

She arched into his touch and tugged at the ridiculous orange-and-white swimsuit that he'd worn to bed, but it was going to be a piece of clothing that held a wonderful memory. Every time she saw him wear it, she'd think of this night and so would he.

With every brush of his bare skin against hers, the desire built, and she completely forgot she was supposed to be telling him about her wishes. At this point their bodies were saying so much more than their words ever could. Maybe someday she'd find a way to capture this feeling with words, but tonight was all about connecting.

A thin slice of morning sunshine slipped through a crack in the hotel room curtains and shone across the foot of the bed and her foot next to his. With her arm across his torso and her head resting on his bare chest, the steady thump-thump of Liam's heart soothed her. For the first time in ages, she had not awakened alone, and it made her ache for so many lost years of intimacy. Nicole's eyes were adjusting to the dim light, and even with the hint of morning stubble shadowing his jawline, she could see hints of the young boy she'd grown up with.

Liam's breathing changed, and although he didn't open his eyes, the faintest hint of a smile formed on his full lips. His hand started a slow path up the length of her arm, around the curve of her shoulder and then down her back.

She shivered, arching against his side and loving the way his fingertips drew small circles on the sensitive skin of her lower back. "Good morning."

"It certainly is." He tipped up her chin and studied her face. "How are you feeling?"

With her fingers tracing the ridges of muscles across his chest, she kissed him softly. "I am feeling fabulous. If this is a dream, don't wake me up."

"I think I'm finally awake for the first time." He brushed her hair back from her face. "My whole life you've been right here, and I was blind to this amazing connection between us, but you knew. Thank you for waking me up."

A nostalgic peacefulness settled in the center of her. "You are very welcome. I wonder what condition the roads are in and if it's safe to travel?"

He propped up on one elbow, smiling down at her. "I don't know what's going on outside, but in here it's most definitely too hot for ice."

"If by some chance we are stuck inside with nowhere to go, what shall we do?" Her foot trailing up the side of his leg hinted at her suggestion.

"I'd like to take another exploratory trip around your beautiful body." He punctuated his wish with a kiss on her shoulder.

"Sign me up for that trip." Every inch of her skin was suddenly sensitive and craving his touch. "Speaking of ice, it's too bad we can't freeze time and stay in this room for a few days."

"Even when we leave this room, it doesn't mean what we have is over. Does it?"

"No. I don't want it to be over. I've waited…" She'd almost said a lifetime, but that sounded over the top. "I've waited a long time for this to happen between us."

On the drive home, they could talk about how to handle the shift in their relationship. Right now, she wanted to continue to play out this fantasy a little while longer before they let the real world creep back into their lives.

Cradling her cheek, he kissed her forehead, the tip of her nose and then her lips. "Let's not check the weather just yet."

"Sounds good to me."

After another hour in bed, they moved to the shower—together this time. She ordered room service so they had an excuse to stay secluded for just a little while longer. Breakfast in bed was so much more fun than sitting in a restaurant. Liam once again proclaimed nothing was as good as her cooking.

His words from the night before floated pleasantly through her mind. *Culinary school was well worth whatever you paid for it.*

Plenty of people had said nice things and complimented her baking and cooking, but no one had said *the* words she had needed to hear for so long. No one had said that the money she'd spent on culinary school was worth it. Her husband, who should have been her biggest supporter, had only said the opposite.

Liam had somehow known to say the exact words that she needed to hear. Words that began to heal the little wounded pieces inside her. Was he too good to be true, or could this man help put her back together, and help her find the woman she'd been once upon a time?

The good news—and bad—was that the roads were safe for travel. They got dressed and packed up the few things they had. His swimsuit and her Welcome to Texas shirt would forever hold great memories.

They started for home a few minutes after checkout time. Since it was Sunday, the bookstore and bistro were closed, but as usual, she had a bakery case to fill with homemade goodies. The drive to San Antonio had been bursting with excited tension and pent-up desire, but the drive home had a different vibe. There was still a ton of sexual tension, but this time it was because they knew how good they could be together.

"When you introduced me to your editor friend, Rebecca, she said something about encouraging you to get back on social media. I know you have an aversion to it, but what is the story with that?"

"I hate being in the public eye." He put on his blinker and changed lanes.

"I don't remember you being this secretive or introverted as a teenager."

"I wasn't. It's because of a social media fiasco."

"A fiasco? What in the world happened?"

His sigh was weary. "It started with a controversial book I edited and then something I said was taken completely out of context. It started with one message that went viral, and no one wanted to hear the boring truth. I guess a scandal, even if it's a fabricated one, is more exciting to some people."

"That is horrible." She took a sip of her coffee and then put it back in the cup holder. "That's why you don't have any social media accounts using your name?"

"Yes. The only thing I have is the Sip & Read website."

"What happened next? Did it just eventually die out?"

"It did, but it could happen again, or someone could dredge up the old stuff and give it new life. I don't want to take the risk."

"I can certainly understand that." She squeezed his shoulder. "So, that is why I heard Travis talking about doing social media promo for the bookstore."

"Yes. I'm letting him do some, and we will see how it goes."

"Teenagers are good at that stuff."

Liam had to hit the brakes hard when a car swerved out of its lane without looking, and the container of car snacks slid onto the floor. "Oh, shoot. Did they spill?"

"No." She picked it up. "The lid stayed on. No pastry emergency today."

"Do you think that hotel where we stayed has a pastry chef?"

"I think they probably do." Was he hinting at the fact that she didn't have to leave the state to have a career? Could she find a good job closer to Oak Hollow?

"How should we handle the new development in our relationship once we get home?" He flicked on his blinker to merge into the highway traffic.

"That's a good question, and something I've been wondering about as well."

"When Jane asked me for a divorce, I can't say it was a huge surprise, but what I did not see coming or suspect was the fact that she was already seeing someone else."

"Oh, no. I'm sorry. Was it the doctor she is now married to?"

"Yes. He'd been to our house, and I knew him. Travis knew him. Me knowing was bad enough, but worse than that was what it did to our son. When people saw that she was dating immediately after filing for divorce, and long before it was finalized, there was talk. Travis heard it and was embarrassed."

"Oh, that sweet boy. I'm so sorry he had to deal with something like that."

"It happened to us in a big city, and with Oak Hollow being a small town…"

"There will be small-town gossip." She finished the thought for him. "And I'm a recent widow."

"Exactly. I don't want our involvement to affect you or Katie or Travis in any negative way."

"Or you or the bookstore." She reached for his hand, and he squeezed her fingers with a calming strength that she needed so much in this moment. "What should we do?"

"I don't want to cheapen what we have, because there is nothing cheap or wrong about it, but do you think keeping our relationship a secret for now is the best idea?"

"Yes. I think you are right." They could ease people into the idea of them being more than friends.

"It's going to be a tough, but necessary until we feel out the situation a bit more."

"We can make it fun. Secret rendezvous to the rooftop garden or you can always climb the tree to my bedroom window," she said.

"Don't think I won't do that." He brought their joined hands to his lips and kissed her knuckles. "This might actually be fun."

Chapter Sixteen

The day was still cold, but the sun had melted any remaining ice from the night before. Liam drove straight to Nicole's house so she could change clothes before going into the bistro kitchen to bake for the upcoming days. The electric company's truck was still in front of his mom's house, so he went inside with Nicole to see if his family was still there.

"Mommy, you're home." The little girl jumped up from the couch where she'd been watching TV and hugged her mom's waist.

"Hi, Katie Cat." She kissed the top of her daughter's head.

Katie surprised Liam by giving him a hug around the waist as well. He had not had the chance to know

Katie very well over the years, but he was hit with a sudden rush of fatherly affection.

"Hey, Dad," Travis said as he walked into the room from the kitchen.

"Hi, kiddo. What's going on this morning?"

"The electricity is back on here, but not at Abuela's. A tree limb took down a power line running from the street to the house, but they are working on it now."

"We saw the trucks when we drove up."

"I'm glad you two are home safe," Mimi said as both of their mothers joined them in the living room.

"Thank you for listening to us and staying in San Antonio for the night." His mama reached up to pat his cheek.

Katie was bouncing with her normal full-speed level of energy, and her inquisitive mind was ready with questions. "Where did you sleep last night, Mommy?"

Liam inhaled too sharply and coughed into his fist. He couldn't look at Nicole for fear they might give themselves away. But he caught the shared smile between their mothers, and if their expressions told him anything, it was that he and Nicole had at least two people who would not be upset about the shift in their relationship.

Without glancing in his direction, Nicole straightened her daughter's ponytail. "We had to stay in the hotel where the conference was being held."

"Cool," Katie said. "Hotels are so much fun."

"I smell coffee," Liam said, and immediately headed for the kitchen in the pretense of needing caffeine. He had certainly enjoyed his night in a hotel. He'd barely had two sips before the whole group followed him into the kitchen.

Katie was still in question mode. "Did you learn more about writing your book?"

"I sure did," Nicole said. "I have a few new ideas about how to make my story better."

Liam took another sip of coffee and then handed his cup to Nicole. "I better get home and check on the bookstore. Travis, do you want to come with me or stay here?"

"I'll go with you. I took some weather photos yesterday, and I want to edit them and print a few. I'm also going to email some of them to the TV station because they sometimes show viewer photographs on the newscast. Maybe they'll pick one of mine."

"That's a great idea," he said to his son. "I bet they will."

"Can I go to the bookstore, too?" Katie asked. "I like being there when it's closed. It's like my own private library. You're so lucky to live above it."

Liam smiled at her. She was reminding him of himself a little more each day. A girl after his own heart. "Of course. If it's okay with your mommy."

"Sure," Nicole said. "I need to change into

clothes I can bake in, and I'll meet you all there in a little while."

He wanted so badly to touch or kiss her before she went upstairs to change, but he shoved his hands in his coat pockets instead. With the intense attraction between them, even the simplest of friendly touches would probably give them away. Keeping this secret was going to be even harder than he'd anticipated.

"The kids have already eaten, but do you need anything to eat before you go?" Mimi asked him.

"No, thank you. We already ate. Mama, are you staying over here until your electricity is back on?"

"Yes. We are going to do a bit of sewing together."

"Sounds good. Come on kids. Get your coats and let's head out."

With the kids, he drove the few miles to the town square. Katie talked most of the way, telling him about their night playing games and telling stories in front of the fireplace, but Liam was having trouble focusing on what the little girl was saying. Thankfully his son was picking up the slack in the conversation.

Once he parked in the back of his building, Travis went straight up to the apartment and his computer to work on his photographs. Katie went to the children's section, and he stood in the center of his bookstore trying to figure out what came next for him. For them.

All four of them.

Needing to keep his hands and mind busy, he went to the storeroom and brought out several large boxes of new books that had just arrived. He'd get them shelved, and that would be one thing marked off his list.

While he worked, most of his thoughts were focused on his night with Nicole. They fit so perfectly in so many ways. Their connection was clear in the way she touched him, as if she could read his thoughts and had been sent to fulfill all his fantasies. She seemed to be able to read his mind, knowing how he like to be touched. And when they had talked after making love, he had learned things about her that he'd never known. She liked bubble baths, long bike rides and sleeping under the stars, all things he would love to do with her very soon.

There was no doubt he was going to have trouble fighting his need to touch and kiss her every time they were around other people. They had turned a corner and gone down a one-way street in their relationship, and there was no going back to the friends-only that they'd been before.

He'd been stocking a bookshelf in the self-help section for about fifteen minutes when Katie came up to him with an open book. "What's up, kiddo?"

"What's a pro...prolo...?"

"Prologue?"

"Yes. That's it."

"It tells you what happened before the story started. A bit of history."

"Oh, the past. I like that idea. I always wonder what happened before." She walked away with her open book, reading aloud.

She was such a little bookworm. Nicole had raised a wonderful daughter, and now he knew that she had done it all on her own. Not only without Jeff's help but in spite of it. That got Liam thinking about his past with Nicole. If their childhood as neighbors was their prologue, that meant there was still a lot of their story left to be written. Lots of life to live. But how much of it would be together? It was up to them to direct the narrative and be the authors of their own lives.

They were in charge of where their choices took them and where their story went from this moment forward. The past was only the prologue of their lives.

That evening, the grandmothers picked up the kids for an event at the church and once again, Liam and Nicole were alone.

While she stood at the sink drying her hands, he slipped up behind her and wrapped his arms around her waist. "Do you want to have a glass of wine on the rooftop before you go home?"

"I'd love to." Turning in his arms, she encircled

his neck and gave him the kiss he'd been craving for hours. "Just let me grab my jacket."

"I'll get the wine." Her quick authentic smile made his tense muscles relax.

As they walked through the apartment, she grabbed a jewel-toned quilt off the back of the couch. The night was clear, and billions of stars twinkled above. He set two glasses of wine on the little table between the chairs and made a mental note to buy something they could sit on together without the distance between them.

"Can we push the two lounge chairs together?" she asked.

"Are you reading my mind?"

She laughed, a musical sound that traveled up and down the scale. "No, but sometimes we do tend to think alike."

He hoped that was true, and that they were one step closer to her realizing she could stay in Oak Hollow and still be successful. And happy. He quickly rearranged the patio furniture and waited for her to sit first. When he eased down beside her, she unfurled the colorful handmade quilt with a shake of her wrists and then covered both of them in a shared pocket of warmth.

Nestled together under infinite stars and unexplored galaxies, there was nowhere else he wanted to be. He knew he was falling too hard and too fast, but trying to stop this between them was next to impossible. He'd have better luck stopping a runaway stallion.

"What would the weather be like if we were in Montana right now?"

"February is usually the month with the highest snowfall, and we would not be on this rooftop with only our light jackets on."

"I wouldn't mind being somewhere cold with you. It's nice and cozy under this blanket." He punctuated the point by sliding his hand under her shirt.

"I'd say we are pretty good at heating things up. A secluded cabin in the snowy mountains could be a lot of fun."

"Count me in."

"Walking in the snow is nice, but I prefer a walk in the spring rain."

"Rain is a lot easier to come by in Texas."

When she hooked one leg across his and looked at him with desire in her green eyes, he held her a little tighter and kissed her lips that were stained with red wine and sweetly yielding under his.

When side by side was no longer enough, she straddled his lap without breaking their kiss, but her knee slipped between the two chairs, sending hers scooting sideways across the wooden decking.

He caught her hips before she could fall and groaned when her shifting movements against his lap created a wave of pleasure. "I'm definitely going to invest in an outdoor futon or double lounger to put up here."

"Good idea. How long do we have until the kids get back?"

Liam glanced at his watch. "A little over an hour. You know…that's more than enough time to give you a tour of my bedroom."

"Now who's the one reading minds? Show me."

She hopped off his lap with the eagerness he remembered from her years ago. It was such a relief to see her coming back to her happy self a little more each day, and her enthusiasm made him chuckle. "You got it."

Hand in hand, they hurried down to the apartment. He tossed the quilt onto the couch and led her down the short hallway to his bedroom but didn't bother with turning on the lights. A shared urgency consumed them, and they fell onto the mattress, grasping one another's clothes, kissing every exposed bit of skin as the clothes fell away.

Last night in the hotel room, they'd made love slowly, with tender caresses and ultimate care and attention to the other's reactions. Whispering encouragements. Sharing. Exploring.

But now, they were wild and uninhibited, making up for all the lost time. All the nights and days they'd each spent alone and lonely.

"More, Liam."

"What do you need, sweetheart?"

With her hands grasping his shoulders, she trembled. "Everything."

He rolled them until he was braced above her. His sweet Nicole was naked and willing in his arms, burning him up and showing him a side of her he'd never known. She made love with an eagerness that left him breathless and aching for more. With another deep, searching kiss, he granted her request and gave her all of himself, body and heart.

His soul wasn't far behind. A consuming passion that left him wide open and vulnerable in a way he'd sworn never to be again.

When the urgency to connect eased, he let himself take in every sensation. Her breath caressing his skin. The sound of her soft sighs. After they'd exhausted one another in the most delicious ways and run out of time, she reluctantly left his arms and started to get dressed.

Liam put his linked hands behind his head. "I just need to look at you and commit this moment to memory, and then I'll get dressed and walk you out."

Before he could get up, she sat on the edge of the bed and laid her hand on his chest. "Stay here in bed. Just like you are. I want to picture you naked with your hair messed up from my hands. She leaned down and kissed him once more. "Good night," she whispered against his lips.

"I'll see you in the morning, sweetheart."

"Yes, you will. Sleep well." She blew a kiss and then slipped out of his bedroom door.

The sheet would soon grow cold beside him, but the beautiful memory of her warm and willing in his bed would forever remain in his mind.

He waited until he heard the sound of her feet on the stairs. Travis would be home soon, so he got up and dressed and went to the kitchen for a snack. A few minutes later, a car pulled up behind the building, and he went to the window to watch his son unlock and come in the back door of the kitchen.

"Did you have fun?" he asked as Travis hung his coat on a hook by the door.

"It was okay."

"Were there any kids you know in the youth group?"

"One girl who sits beside me in history class."

The teenager ducked his head, but Liam caught the grin his son was trying to hide. "That's cool." He knew better than to push the issue or ask too many questions about a girl. He'd get more if he waited for him to be ready to share.

"I'm going to take a shower and go to bed," Travis said.

"Good night, son."

"Night, Dad."

Liam got a drink, made sure everything was locked up for the night and went back to his bed. The vanilla scent of Nicole still hung in the sweetness of the air, but the sheets were cold without her beside him. He fell asleep with his mind replaying events and conversations and contemplating one thought.

How could he keep her in his bed and his life?

Chapter Seventeen

Over the next week, Nicole and Liam got in the habit of taking their lunch break together, either in his locked office or up in the apartment. And occasionally on the rooftop. One day, someone tried to open his office door when they were in a compromising situation. And they were pretty sure Amy saw them kissing in the kitchen. Thankfully, no one seemed to be the least bit concerned about them being a couple.

Nicole had just finished baking a batch of cookies and was coming out of the walk-in cooler when Liam came into the kitchen. "You missed lunch while you were on your conference call. Are you hungry?"

"I am starving."

"There is only a little bit more of the tomato basil soup I made. Do you want a taste before it's all gone?"

He came close enough to brush his knuckles over her cheek. "Do you know what I want more than the last bite of soup?"

"What's that? The last brown butter pecan cookie?"

"No." He moved in so close she could feel the heat of his body. "Something even sweeter than that."

"Tell me." Her voice sounded breathless like she'd been running a race rather than just standing at the kitchen island.

"I'd rather show you." He pressed her back against the door of the walk-in cooler and barely had his lips on hers when they heard footsteps on the stairs.

"Dad, are you down there?"

"Rain check?" he said in a husky whisper as he stepped away from her.

"You got it." The anticipation of when that would happen was part of the fun.

The winter evening was clear and mild. The perfect kind of night for sitting around the firepit on the rooftop and roasting marshmallows. Nicole sat beside Liam on one side and the kids were across from them.

Travis rooted through the s'mores supplies basket. "Where is the chocolate? I don't see it in here."

"Oh, I remember setting it down somewhere…" Nicole drummed her fingers on her knee. "But I don't remember where. I'll go retrace my steps and find it. Anyone need anything else while I'm down there?"

"I could use another mug of your spiced cider with rum," Liam said.

"You got it." His half grin sent a tingle to parts low on her body, reminding her of the last time they had made love in his bed. Nicole leaned in her chair and kissed Liam square on the mouth. When she braced her hands on the arms of her chair to stand, Katie and Travis were staring at them—him with his eyes wide as silver dollars and her daughter's little mouth drawn into an O. That's when Nicole realized what she had done.

"Oops," she whispered under her breath. So much for their relationship remaining a secret.

"Mommy, is Liam your boyfriend?" The little girl's surprise had turned into a huge smile.

Nicole cut a glance toward Liam, afraid he'd be upset that she'd blown their secret without talking to him first, but his expression matched Katie's.

"Guess that secret is out," Liam said with a chuckle. "How do the two of you feel about us dating?" he asked the kids.

Katie bounced in her chair. "I think it's great."

"I'm cool with it," Travis said, and skewered another marshmallow. "It's not like I didn't have my suspicions. You two are worse than teenagers."

Nicole and Liam glanced at one another and then laughed. They'd been joking that they were acting like teens in the backs of cars and climbing trees, and apparently there was some truth to it.

"So, now that you two know, we need to talk about what happens next," Nicole said.

"That's right. Travis, remember how it was when your mom and I started our divorce?"

The teen grimaced. "You mean the talk about mom moving on too quick?"

"Yes. That's why we haven't shared this with anyone yet."

"You don't want people to talk because…" Travis glanced at Nicole like he wasn't sure what was okay to say.

"Because I am a widow," she said. "There might be people who think it's too soon for me to be dating anyone."

"I don't think it's too soon," Katie said. "Liam makes you smile more than daddy ever did."

A little piece of Nicole's heart shriveled. Why had she stayed with Jeff for so long? It had set a bad example.

"Mommy, I think Mimi will be happy, and I think Abuela will be happy, too."

And now her daughter was calling Liam's mom by the Spanish name for grandmother? Her pulse raced, and she was starting to freak out just a little bit. Why wasn't Liam freaking out?

"I think you are right, Katie Cat," Liam said. "They will both be very happy."

Katie waved her marshmallow over the flames. "Do we have to keep keeping it a secret from everyone else?"

"We don't need to go around telling anyone who isn't family, but it doesn't have to stay a secret." A wave of relief eased some of the tension Nicole hadn't even realized she was holding. She'd kept so many embarrassing secrets about her marriage, she didn't want to do that again. "I'll go and look for the chocolate now."

She went downstairs and paused in the center of Liam's apartment. What happened now that the kids knew about their relationship? And what would happen if she got one of the jobs she'd applied for and they had to leave town? Her daughter loved it here. Katie was bonding with Liam, and Nicole was bonding with Travis. The four of them had become a sort of…family unit.

In the span of a few minutes, she and Liam had gone from secret love affair to girlfriend and boyfriend. Was there a job out there that was worth giving all this up? She was starting to think that there was not.

Still, she also knew all too well how something

that started great could end up in a disaster that broke hearts and ruined lives.

But this is Liam.

She turned and took a step with the intentions of pulling Liam aside to talk this through, but she stopped and sat on the arm of the couch. She could not let her libido and emotions rush her into a decision that would affect the rest of her life. The rest of *all* their lives.

Her romance with Liam was new and exciting. And scary. She braced a hand on the back of the couch. She just needed to take a breath and some time to think things through. It was too early on in their relationship to discuss a long-term future. She needed to think and plan, because right now, her mind was too jumbled with clashing ideas. Go or stay. Continue to fight for a high-profile career or give up that dream and chase a new one?

There was no rush to figure it out tonight. She had time to make smart decisions.

If she and Katie stayed in Oak Hollow, and her relationship with Liam became even more serious that was one thing, but what if she gave up a great job to stay and it didn't work out between them? If she stopped pursuing a professional culinary career, would it prove she had wasted her money on school, or...

Would it prove she was smart enough to make up

her mind for herself? Nicole smiled as more tension eased from her muscles.

She spotted the chocolate bars on the apartment's kitchen counter. After a few calming breaths, she grabbed the candy, and as she made her way up to the rooftop, she heard her daughter's cheery mile-a-minute voice.

"I like being like a family," Katie said.

Nicole froze in place with her hand clasped to her mouth. She might need to do her thinking a little faster than she'd planned.

Chapter Eighteen

The next day was Sunday, and to give Nicole a break from cooking, Liam and the kids had suggested lunch at the Acorn Café. While she waited in the sunshine outside the front doors of Sip & Read for the three of them, she checked her email on her phone. There was nothing from Hamilton Resorts, and in that moment, she made a plan. She would wait another couple of weeks to see if she heard back from them. If she didn't hear anything in that time frame, that would be her sign to talk to Liam about them staying permanently in Oak Hollow.

Nicole felt a buoyancy that made her raise up on her toes, much like her daughter did when she was excited. Last night, she had taken the time to remind Katie that they had only come to stay temporarily. She had listened, but Nicole didn't think she'd truly heard or believed that moving away was still a possibility. Less and less of one each day, but still it was there.

Katie was the first one out the door followed by the guys. "We're ready to go eat."

"I'm going to run ahead of everyone and grab a table." Travis jogged a few steps then looked over his shoulder. "Booth or table?"

"Booth, please," Liam said. "The kids helped me set up the new book display."

"Good job." Her daughter took her hand, and the man who made her as giddy as a schoolgirl walked on her other side. What would he do if she reached out and held his hand in public? What would the townsfolk do? A few people had made comments about them being cute together, but no one had seemed shocked or started any gossip.

They walked across the center of the town square to the 1950s-style diner that sat at one corner and had been a staple in this town long before she'd been born. Travis had chosen a booth by the front windows that looked out over the center of the square. The seats were covered with turquoise faux leather, and she sat beside Liam.

"We used to come here all the time before you started cooking for us," Travis said, and passed out the menus that were tucked behind a wire rack of condiments. "I'm having the chicken-fried steak."

"That's always been a favorite of mine, and as a chef, I give the food here an A-plus. That's probably what I'll end up getting, too." The restaurant served Southern cooking that ranged from fried chicken and pot pies to a variety of unique burger options.

"I'm getting a cheeseburger and french fries," Katie said.

"Me, too." Liam closed his menu. The front cover featured a gorgeous tree of life that had been painted by Alexandra Walker, because this was her uncle Sam Hargrove's café.

Mrs. Suarez, who had been Liam's and Nicole's high school science teacher, stopped beside their table. "Hello, everyone. I just wanted to stop by and tell you how much I've been enjoying your pastries. We usually buy a variety and bring them home to have with our morning coffee."

"Thank you so much. I'm so glad to hear that." She never got tired of the compliments.

"It's so nice to see young people come home to Oak Hollow, and we are certainly glad you've brought your talent for us to enjoy." The older woman pointed back and forth between her and Liam. "I remember you two were always such good friends, and you make an even cuter couple."

Nicole wasn't sure how to respond, but Mrs. Suarez was too busy talking to need a response.

"And such adorable children. I've got a few more people to say hello to. Y'all enjoy your dinner."

"You, too, Mrs. Suarez," Liam said as she waved enthusiastically to someone across the café and hurried away.

"See, Mommy. No one thinks it's bad that you are girlfriend and boyfriend."

Liam laced his fingers with hers and kissed her cheek. "I think she is right."

"It does appear that way." Leaning her head against his shoulder, Nicole let herself relax and enjoy the moment she was in.

That evening, she wanted to try out a small batch of a new recipe. Although it was actually a very old one. Liam's mom had given it to her and told her all about her grandmother from Puerto Rico who had passed it along. Nicole was going to surprise Liam with it because it was one of his favorites.

A country music radio station Nicole had grown to like was playing on low volume, and she had all of the ingredients laid out on the center island of the bistro's kitchen. The current song was about moonlight dancing in a lover's eyes, and it made her think of sitting on the roof with Liam. It had become one of their favorite places.

Travis pushed slowly through the swinging door into the kitchen with his phone held out in front of him like he so often did, especially since he'd taken on the job of promoting Sip & Read, since Liam had a strong dislike for social media. He'd been more than happy for his son to do it.

"This is the bistro's kitchen, and this is the pastry chef who bakes some of the best food in the whole Texas Hill Country."

Surprised by his compliment, she smiled and waved at the camera. He had to get approval from Liam before posting anything, so she wasn't worried about him filming her.

"Will you tell us what you are making today?" he asked.

"I am getting things ready to make your abuela's recipe for quesitos. They are a delicious cream cheese puff pastry that is popular in Puerto Rico where your great-great-grandmother was from."

"So, it's a family recipe. That's major cool."

The word "family" swirled in her head and brought back thoughts that were never far from the front of her mind.

What is next for us?

He stopped recording and lowered his phone to his side. "Can I for real film you making these? The whole process."

"Sure. But I don't know how many people looking for a bookstore will be interested in my baking."

"I'm going to start promoting the bistro, too. And I'm building content that could eventually be a podcast or something on the internet. Just think, you could even end up having your own cooking show someday."

A slow smile built along with a burst of adrenaline. "That is something I've never thought about, but I'm intrigued." Was it possible people would someday know her name? Not just other chefs or people in the culinary world but everyday people.

"Don't do anything else until I get set up." Taking the stairs two at a time, Travis raced up to the apartment.

She pictured some of the famous chefs she'd grown up watching on TV. While other kids had been interested in cartoons or popular sitcoms, she'd been watching old episodes of Julia Child and a whole list of others. They were the chefs who had encouraged her to chase her dreams, but she had never even considered having her own cooking show.

She followed him upstairs to check her hair and makeup. Liam and Katie were sitting at the kitchen table. He was working on his laptop, and her daughter was writing in a notebook. They both smiled at her, and her chest filled with warmth. "You two look very busy."

"We're writing books," Katie said. "Mine is a kid's story about a grumpy rhinoceros."

"Where did that idea come from?" Liam asked.

"From Travis being grumpy." She giggled and put her hand to her mouth.

"Not funny," Travis said as he came out of his bedroom. "I'm not grumpy."

"But you were when I first met you, and by the end of my story, Grumpus Arumpus the Rhinoceros won't be grumpy either. I'll dedicate it to you."

Travis's grin made him look so much like his father had at the same age. "You better dedicate it to me. I'm going to be filming Nicole baking so you two don't come downstairs and interrupt the video."

"You know I won't come down there and risk being in the video," Liam said.

Nicole squeezed Liam's shoulder. "Well, I need to make sure I am ready for my starring role." She grabbed her travel makeup bag from her purse and went into the bathroom. She redid her hair into a neater bun low on the back of her head. With another coat of mascara and pink lip gloss, she felt more camera ready.

Back down in the kitchen, Travis had set up the new tripod he'd bought with the money he'd earned while helping her bake. "I'm ready whenever you are."

She started baking and narrating every step of the process and telling bits of cooking trivia along the way. It was a lot more fun than she thought it would be. Once she had put the quesitos into the oven, he stopped the camera.

"How did I do?" she asked him.

"Great. You really should think about having

your own cooking show. If it's on the internet, there is always the chance of getting famous."

"I will definitely give it some serious thought. Thank you, Travis." She was kind of loving this new idea. She could potentially put her culinary skills to use not only here at the bistro but also across the world on the internet. Could that be the success she hoped for?

When Valentine's Day rolled around, their moms decided it would be a good idea for them to take the kids to San Antonio to the zoo and stay for the night. Liam knew they were giving him and Nicole the chance to spend time alone together, and he was 100 percent on board with that plan.

With a bottle of wine he had picked out from the wine bar downstairs, he met Nicole on the rooftop. "I have the white wine."

"That one is perfect,"

The bright smile she shot his way never failed to bring a similar one to his own mouth, and as usual, he couldn't resist kissing her. She was so beautiful with her hair down around her shoulders. A form-fitting soft red sweater hugged her body, much like he longed to do.

"Let's eat before it gets cold," she said.

They sat across from one another at the iron table and ate, drank and laughed. When the sunset slipped below the horizon, the temperature dropped, and they'd moved their Valentine's celebration to his bedroom.

He turned on the bedroom lamp and kicked off his shoes. "Since you cooked for me, I'm going to give you a massage."

"That sounds fabulous. I've never had a guy give me a massage before."

"I'm glad I can be the first." He was glad, but he was also surprised. This woman deserved to be pampered. He rubbed the palms of his hands together. "Get naked and comfortable, sweetheart."

"If I get naked, are you going to be able to concentrate on a massage?" she said with a laugh, and pulled her sweater over her head.

Her bra was red lace, and there wasn't much of it. He loved it. "That's a good question. It depends. Do your panties match your sexy bra?"

"Hmm. Let's find out."

He leaned against the wall with his arms crossed over his chest, feeling like the luckiest man in the entire world.

She made a slow, teasing production of unzipping and wiggling her jeans slowly over her hips and down her legs. After blowing him a kiss, she stretched out on her stomach, unhooked her bra and glanced over her shoulder with a sultry grin. "I'm ready for you."

He chuckled and yanked off his shirt then straddled her legs and squeezed massage oil into the palm of his hand. "If you keep being this seductive, your massage won't last long." He smoothed the oil over her soft skin, and her moan almost undid him. He held out as long as he could, but her a massage ended with both of them being very satisfied.

When Liam came back from the kitchen with ice water, Nicole was looking over the editing notes he'd made on the most recent chapter of her book. He climbed back in bed beside her. She had the sheet drawn up to barely cover her breasts, looking so tempting. Even though he'd made love to her only a few minutes ago, he wanted her again.

Nicole put the pages on her lap, leaned back on the bed and chewed on the end of her pen. "If I submit my writing to the publisher you work for, should I mention or not mentioned that you have been helping me and editing my work? Will knowing that affect my chances?"

He rolled to his side and then slipped his hand under the sheet to stroke the silky skin of her bare thigh. "I'm not a big name enough for it to matter that much."

"I think you are being modest. I've seen the awards on the bookshelf in your office. At least three or four of them."

"I've done okay. Nic, you don't need to use my name. You are good enough to get a contract all on your own."

"You really think so? You know when I do something, I like to do it to the best of my ability until I get it right."

"Oh, yes, I'm very aware." He admired her determination, but he did still worry because her drive for success reminded him of his ex a little more than he was comfortable with. "Every time I give you notes, you really take everything to heart and make it better. If you keep working and learning at this rate, you'll be published before you know it. Pretty soon, you won't have any free time between being a baking genius, writing and being a cooking show star."

Leaning his way, she kissed the top of his shoulder. "I'll always make time for you. And I'm not counting on the cooking show thing. It's probably just going to be something fun Travis and I can do together."

When she said motherly things like that, it really made him hopeful for their future. "You know, you spend more time with him than his mother does when she is in town. I'm hoping he will want to stay here with me even when she gets back from her field placement."

"I hope he does, too. In the time I've been here, I have seen him adjusting and enjoying himself. When we cook together, he talks more about school and other kids."

"He is laughing and smiling more. I think I've

found someone in town who is willing to work with him on his photography."

"That's good news. Does Travis know yet?"

"No. I'll talk to him about it tomorrow."

"You are such a good daddy. I wish Katie had had a daddy like you."

Liam's heart did a funny little stutter, in a good way. He could see himself being her stepdad, but when he considered voicing that thought, he bit down on the inside of his cheek. It was too soon for a conversation that serious.

Nicole tossed the pages she'd been editing to the foot of the bed and draped herself across him. "This is something I never thought I'd be doing."

"What's that? Writing a book?"

"That plus being naked in bed with you while I edit my work."

"I am becoming a big fan of naked editing. And there is no one else I want to do it with." He kissed her lips and was working his way down her neck. "But I'm not sure how much work we will actually get done if we make this a habit."

"That's the truth."

When he lifted her to straddle his hips, the pages slipped one by one off the foot of the bed and onto the floor. The romance happening in their real life was definitely more urgent and satisfying.

"I'm so glad you are my writing partner," she

whispered against his lips. "I wouldn't be able to do this with Ivy Moon."

With his lips on the curve of her breast, he momentarily froze.

I need to find a good time to tell her.

One evening later that week, the four of them had just finished eating dinner together at the kitchen table in his apartment, and Travis was clearing the dishes.

"Aha." Nicole snapped her fingers. "I know what happens in my next chapter. I have to write it down."

Liam chuckled. "Go grab a notebook or your laptop." He knew the urgency to get ideas written down before any of the thoughts drifted away to that place where they swirled with others and were lost in a sea of words.

"I have homework to finish," Travis said. "I'll be in my bedroom."

Nicole sat on Liam's emerald green sectional couch with her laptop.

Since she had cooked, Liam was washing dishes and Katie stood beside him, drying each dish as he handed it to her.

"What are you going to do with that room at the end of the hall with all the boxes in it?" Katie asked Liam.

"It was supposed to be my office, but I tend to either use the big office downstairs or work at the kitchen table. Do you have an idea of what I should do with it?"

She worried her teeth along her lower lip. "It could be a third bedroom."

"It's kind of small but I guess you're right." He pointed to a door on the opposite side of the room. "That leads into a lot of unused attic space, and I've thought about expanding the apartment across the whole building."

"You should do that," Katie said with so much enthusiasm that she almost dropped a plate.

"But until then, you think I should turn the little room into a bedroom?"

"Yes. Then Mommy and I could stay over here and not have to always go back to Mimi's house."

The clink of Nicole's fingers on the keyboard came to a sudden halt and she stiffened before her gaze shot to his. They looked at one another across the top of her little girl's head of thick brown hair platted into two long braids.

He cleared his throat. "So, a guest room for you and your mommy?"

She sighed, cocked her head and gave him a look. "You know… I'm not a little kid anymore. I know how things work. You can share a room with each other, and it would be okay."

His throat grew tight, and he had no idea what to say. Thankfully, Nicole put her laptop on the coffee table and came around the island and into the kitchen. It seemed she was also searching for the right words.

"Katie Cat, what has you thinking about this?"

She put down a dish and propped her elbow on the counter. "I love being at Mimi's, but it is really fun to be here. Like a *real* family for the first time."

The little girl's statement seemed to imply that she had never had the "real family" experience. Liam saw Nicole's throat bob, and he could tell she was holding back tears. He moved closer to her and rubbed her back.

He liked Katie's idea, probably way more than he should, but he and Nic had not talked about forever or even next month. It was time for that to change. Once they got through the chaos of the upcoming book fest, he would start that conversation.

Chapter Nineteen

The day before the book festival, Sip & Read was ready for their big event. Because Valentine's had just past, the whole bookstore had an extra bit of sparkle thanks to glittery heart garlands and shimmery balloons. Katie had been involved in choosing the holiday decor, and the girl loved glitter. Liam knew they would be vacuuming up the bits of sparkle for weeks, but the store did look nice.

Almost every full-time employee was here today and would be again tomorrow. One group was rearranging furniture and book stands to accommodate rows of seating for the book readings. The bistro was being stocked with extra food, and tomorrow they'd have double the normal staff at the coffee and wine bar and in the kitchen.

This event would bring business to Sip & Read, help the authors attending and hopefully increase business around the whole square, but he just wanted to hide in his apartment or office. As always, he was dreading being in the public eye. Too much attention directed toward him was one of his least favorite things, but the book fest—originally only meant to be a one-time event for the bookstore's opening—was something everyone had come to expect. His town was worth a day or two of discomfort on his part.

He caught sight of Nicole behind the coffee bar, and when she flashed him a smile, he was tempted to whisk her away to the rooftop to hide away from everything and everyone.

What had helped the most with preparing for the book fest was having Nicole and her skill at managing people and events. She had naturally moved into the role of helping him in more areas than just the bistro's kitchen. They were working together as a team. Partners, just like she'd said after the day the bistro reopened. After today, he knew for sure that he wanted to offer her more than just working for him. Part ownership in the bistro would hopefully make her see that she was a successful chef right here in their hometown.

"Liam Mendez," said a voice he knew well. "Get over here and give me a hug."

He turned around just in time to receive a very

enthusiastic hug from author Sara Love. "How are you?" he asked once she'd removed her hold around his rib cage enough that he could breathe.

"I'm so excited to be here. The Texas Hill Country is just as beautiful as you said." Sara was almost six feet tall with a personality to match. Her long, straight blond hair was loose, and she was dressed in black, her signature color.

He looked at his watch. "You got here earlier than I expected."

"I rented a sports car and had so much fun driving through the hills on the twisting roads. I've already checked into my room at the B and B and came right over to see you. The good news is that they are able to accommodate my extra night after all."

"That is good news. I want you to meet someone." Liam glanced back to see if Nic was still at the bar, and then they made their way around the chairs and over to her. "Sara, this is Nicole."

"It's a pleasure to meet you," Sara said.

"You as well. Welcome to Oak Hollow."

"Thanks."

"Can I get you anything to eat or drink?" Nicole offered.

"I would kill for a cappuccino."

"I'll make it," Amy said from the other end of the bar.

Sara bent to look in the bakery case. "Look at

those beautiful pastries. I'm gaining five pounds just looking at them, so I might as well eat one."

Nicole moved behind the case. "Which one would you like?"

"Let's start with that one with the dusting of powdered sugar. Where do you get these?"

"Nicole makes them. She is a very talented pastry chef," Liam said, and liked the smile his compliment put on Nic's lovely face.

She handed a plate to Sara just as Amy finished making the coffee, and then Nicole was called back to the kitchen.

"Excuse me," she said to Sara. "Duty calls."

"I'm sure I'll see you around."

Sara hooked her arm around his, startling him out of watching the woman he'd fallen in love with as she walked away. "Let's find a place to sit while you eat and have your coffee."

"Do you have an office where we can talk? There is a lot of activity going on out here."

"Sure. I'll grab your coffee. Follow me." This boisterous woman usually required a lot of attention and was on the high maintenance side, very unlike his Nic. As expected, the next few days had the potential to be busy and exhausting.

Nicole headed down the back hallway to Liam's office, eager to tell him about the evening she had planned for the two of them. As she drew close, voices filtered down the hallway.

"We have so much more we need to discuss," said Sara Love. "We can make this so amazing for both of us, and then you can come see me in New York more often. Can you do dinner tonight? We can order in, so we have privacy to talk."

The other woman's words tainted the air with a sourness that made Nicole scrunch up her face.

Say no. Tell her you can't have dinner with her.

"I think that will work," Liam said.

Nicole's belly twisted into a tighter knot. She knew Liam was stressed about the big event. She had planned to give him a massage tonight, and then have a quiet evening relaxing and spending time together before the chaos of tomorrow's event. That plan had just been sidelined. If she had already told him about her plans for the evening, would Liam still have said yes to dinner with the woman who looked at him like he was the most delectable chocolate-covered pastry?

She stopped in the open doorway, but they didn't look her way. Liam was sitting on the edge of his desk with his arms crossed over his chest and Sara was standing in front of him, way too close for Nicole's liking. She knocked on the frame of the open door. "Sorry to interrupt."

Liar.

The tall, gorgeous blond who had enthusiastically hugged Liam when she arrived at the bookstore took her hand off his forearm. Her formfitting black dress highlighted her curvaceous body, which would make any man take a second look. Nicole really liked Sara's books, but this did not make her want to read another one, even if they were edited by Liam. "The author from Dallas thinks he'll have trouble being here for his morning reading."

Liam stood and shifted away from Sara then scratched his head. "That's fine. We can move his reading to later in the day."

"I can switch times with him if that helps," Sara said.

Liam returned her big smile. "That would be a big help. Thanks."

"I'm glad that is worked out. Guess I'll get back to the kitchen," she said, and turned to hurry away, but could still hear Sara's voice.

"It's been too long since you came to New York. I can't wait to show you the new restaurant beside my apartment."

"I've been too busy to travel."

Nicole loathed this feeling of jealousy. It was too much like the way Jeff had made her feel before she had decided she didn't care what he did. Before she'd given up on her marriage and made the best of the bad situation that she'd put herself in.

But she didn't want to give up on Liam.

A couple of hours later, the bookstore had closed for the day and Nicole was alone in the kitchen.

Alone with her thoughts that were taking her no-where good. Her and Liam's moms had made plans to take care of the kids while they worked on this event, and Nicole had planned to stay over at the apartment for the night. But now, she wasn't sure if that plan needed to change.

Liam pushed through the swinging door. "How's it going?"

"Fine."

"Then why are you scowling?"

"Am I?"

"Yes." He came closer. "Talk to me."

"I had something planned for us tonight, but I hear that you have other plans for dinner."

"How did you know? I was just coming in here to talk to you about it."

"I heard when I was standing in your open of-fice doorway."

"Oh, yeah. Sara wants to meet so we can talk about publishing stuff."

"Is it an author and editor kind of relationship or something…else."

"Sweetheart, are you jealous?" He pulled her into his arms, trapping her against the heat of his body.

"Maybe. Just a tiny bit."

"You have absolutely nothing to be worried about with Sara."

"Does she know that?"

He grinned and kissed her until she relaxed in

his arms. "I think she knows. I've never given her a reason to believe there can be anything romantic between us."

"She doesn't exactly strike me as a woman who doesn't go after what she wants until she gets it."

"That's true. I'll make it clear tonight that I am not available. After I have my business meeting with her, can we still do whatever it is you have planned for us?"

"Part of it was dinner, but it sounds like you'll be eating at your business meeting." She wanted to ask where they were meeting but decided against it. She didn't need to appear even more jealous than she already had.

"I was just planning to grab takeout from the Acorn Café and bring it back here."

"To your office?" The thought of Liam and Sara alone in the room where they liked to have private lunches was very unappetizing.

His grin widened. "No. To one of the tables out in the bookstore."

"I guess I can make dinner for y'all," she grudgingly offered.

"I'm not going to ask you to do that. You are still staying over tonight, right?"

"That's the plan."

"Good." He leaned in for one more kiss. "I'm going to go get the food and get this meeting done so you and I can enjoy the evening together. It's not very often we have the apartment to ourselves, and I want to make the most of every minute."

That made her smile and her anxiety ease. "Sounds good. I'm done in here, so I'll be upstairs. Maybe I'll work on my book."

"I'll meet you up there as soon as I can, sweetheart."

She watched him walk from the kitchen and barely resisted the urge to run after him and call out that she loved him. Instead, she stayed where she was.

I love you, Liam.

Chapter Twenty

Sip & Read was ready for the big day, but Liam was not. He was warm in his bed beside the woman he loved, and there was nowhere else he wanted to be. Nicole stretched, making the sheet slip down enough to give him a peek of the curves of her breasts.

"Good morning, sweetheart."

"It sure is." She snuggled against his side.

"Can I just hide up here in the apartment all day? Or better yet, can we just stay in bed until tomorrow?"

She propped up on one elbow. "I'm afraid not, but the day will be over before you know it."

"Promise?"

"What I can promise is that I will be here to help you through this whole event."

He pressed an open palm to his chest where a

comfortable fullness settled inside him. "I like the sound of that." He hoped them working together would become a permanent thing. As soon as they got through today, it would be time for a heart-to-heart discussion because she needed to know how much he loved her. How much she made his days and nights feel new and hopeful with so many possibilities laid out before them.

"You didn't say anything about how your meeting with Sara went last night."

That was not a topic he wanted to think about right now while he was in bed with his Nic. Although it was flattering that she was jealous, he didn't want her to worry about him with other women. Last night, Sara had hinted at what there could be between them, but he had quickly made his intentions, or lack thereof, very clear. Whether she would truly hear him was in doubt because Sara tended to get an idea and think she knew best.

"We got a story idea worked through, and she wasn't surprised to hear that we are dating." His cell phone started ringing, and he groaned. "It's starting already."

The town square was packed with so many visitors that their cars were spilling down neighborhood streets. Other businesses around the square were doing special things for the day as well. Many were having sales, and others were giving various demonstrations. Mackintosh's Five & Dime even had a table of kids' crafts set up near the playground. Beside the gazebo were long white canopy-covered tables, each decorated by an author to showcase their books, which would be autographed and sold to readers.

Liam moved around throughout the day, making sure everything was running smoothly, and thankfully it was. Sales were great for the store and the visiting authors. People were raving about the food, and it was turning out to be a much better day than he'd anticipated. Having more employees this year had helped. He'd stressed about this day for nothing.

It was finally the end of the day, the bookstore had cleared out and he flipped the sign on the front door to Closed. He followed the voices to where Nicole and Sara were talking near the bakery case and coffee bar. Even though he thought it was kind of adorable that Nic was jealous, he was glad the women seemed to be getting along well. They were both going to be in his life—in very different ways—but he didn't want there to be any tension. Sara had seemed disappointed when he told her about his relationship with Nic, but that couldn't be helped.

"Was culinary school hard?" Sara asked, and took another sip of wine.

"It wasn't easy, but when it's something you love, it's worth the extra effort."

"That's true. It's been the same for me with my writing. What have your career goals been?"

Liam paused before rounding the corner, waiting to hear what Nic would say.

"I have been trying to get a position as head pastry chef at a big resort. I'm still waiting to hear back from one of them."

"That's great," Sara said.

Great? That is not great. His belly twisted into a knot.

Instead of joining them, he headed for his office. Nicole's open laptop was on his desk, and when he sat down and moved it to the side, the screen blinked on. It was open to her email, and an unread message caught his eye. He thought he might be sick.

It was from Hamilton Resorts, and the subject line of the email read *We look forward to speaking with you.*

Chapter Twenty-One

The night before when Liam had called Nicole into his office and told her she'd received an email from Hamilton Resorts, he'd done his best to put on a cheery face, but she hadn't been fooled. He was anything but happy, and the rest of the evening he'd been tense and a bit distant, claiming he was only tired.

This was a very pivotal moment in her life. Her marriage had been a wrong turn, but this time, she had to get it right. She'd even considered not setting up an interview, but she had to know, or she would forever wonder. She couldn't *not* take the meeting.

She'd done a bit of morning baking to keep her hands and mind busy while awaiting her afternoon meeting. She couldn't believe they were willing to set up an online meeting on a Sunday afternoon, but the woman had said she liked to do so when possible because it lessened her workload during the week and gave her time for other things. Nicole understood that logic completely because it was exactly what she did. She had a feeling she was going to like this woman.

In the quiet of Liam's office, Nicole set herself up at his desk and opened her laptop. Her scheduled interview would begin in a few minutes, and she would have the answer she'd been seeking for so long. Would Hamilton Resorts offer her the job? And the new question, would she consider taking it if they did?

She looked at two framed photographs on the wall beside the desk. The top one was of Liam at about age ten with his father, and the other was of Liam with Travis at about the same age as he had been in the first one. Fathers and sons, sharing experiences and building bonds. She had that with Katie, but it would be so nice to have that on a bigger scale. A family size scale. Both Mendez men were making a strong impression on their lives. She finally had Liam in her life in a way she'd only dreamed of, and she loved him.

And she loved their life in Oak Hollow.

The alarm on her phone sounded and she jumped. It was time to click into the video Zoom meeting with one of the executives of Hamilton Resorts. The meeting connected, and she sat up straighter in her chair. She saw a woman with black hair smoothed back into a low ponytail, a pale blue blouse that looked fabulous with her dark complexion and a smile that put Nicole at ease.

"Good afternoon, Mrs. Evans. Thank you for agreeing to meet with me on a weekend."

"Not a problem at all. In fact, if I have any flour on my face, it's because I was just in the kitchen of the bistro where I work. I like to take some time on Sundays to get a few things done."

The executive's smile broadened. "That's exactly the kind of thing we like to hear about an employee's work ethic."

After a few minutes of pleasantries, they got down to business. There were questions, and she shared her past experiences and what she was currently doing. She told her about reopening the bistro within less than a week, and how she had increased the business well beyond what it had ever been before.

"That's very impressive, Mrs. Evans. It's a great success story."

"Thank you so much."

The bistro is successful, and I made it happen.

What she was doing right here in Oak Hollow *was* being successful. Everyone was happy. Liam was the perfect example of how a healthy relationship should look. What was better than a man who was loving and caring and patient and honest?

"I would like to offer you a head pastry chef po-sition."

Nicole's heart seemed to pause for a beat and then pounded hard enough to make her gasp. "Oh, my goodness. Thank you so much." These were the words that she had been waiting to hear since her first day of culinary school. Right here in this mo-ment, she had accomplished that goal. Spending money on culinary school had *not* been a waste.

"We would also like to offer you a choice be-tween two locations. One of the resorts is in the Colorado Springs area and the other is near Denver. Do you have a preference?"

"Oh, wow. I didn't expect to have a choice. This is wonderful."

But is it really?

Nicole's hands were twisting in her lap. She *did* have a choice. A choice between a resort or a fam-ily bistro where everyone was happy.

"Could I have a day or two to talk to my family about it?" She probably thought Nicole meant talk about which location, but what she actually meant was whether to take the job at all.

"Yes, of course. If you could just get back to us by Friday morning, that would be great."

"No problem. I should be able to let you know way before Friday."

"I will send you some information about both locations, and that should help you decide which one will be a better fit for your family."

Family.

The word made something inside of her settle into place. "That would be great. Thank you so much for this opportunity."

They said goodbye, she closed her laptop, and the room went silent except for the whooshing of blood in her ears. "I did it. I accomplished what I set out to do." She laughed. "And now I want something different."

She didn't have to leave a place where they were so happy to be a success. Her idea of what success was had changed without her even realizing it. It wasn't a job title to brag about. It was...

Happiness.

Eager to talk to Liam about staying permanently in Oak Hollow, she pushed against the desk to roll back in the chair, and her foot kicked a stack of file folders on the floor underneath his desk. Leaning down for a look, she discovered three stacks.

"Good grief. Is this his idea of a filing system?" The file cabinet in the back corner must either be full, or he just didn't use it. She couldn't leave everything knocked over, so she got down onto her hands and knees to gather up the ones she had kicked off the top of a stack. A few pages were loose, and when she sat in the chair to see if she could figure out what folder to put them in, the second one caught her attention.

It was a royalty statement from Liam's publisher.

"Wow. That's a lot of money," she whispered.

Did editors get paid royalties? She studied it a little closer, and her breath caught so ragged that she coughed.

Author: Liam Mendez/Ivy Moon.

Book title: Her New Life.

Nicole's skin went cold and pebbled with goose bumps.

Chapter Twenty-Two

Liam sat on his rooftop with his bad mood and
a beer that he wouldn't normally be drinking this
early in the day. The reason was simple and complicated all at the same time. Nicole was in his office having an interview for her dream job. A dream
that would take her away from him. A dream that
was the opposite of his.

When Nicole had read the email aloud, the language had sounded like it was only a formality and
she already had the job. Her excitement had come
quickly. He'd gritted his teeth and smiled for her
benefit, but it gutted him that another woman might
be about to put her career ahead of their relationship. Would a job once again be more important
than being with him? More important than his love?

But I haven't told her that I love her.

Would her knowing change anything? He tipped back the cold bottle and drained the last sip of beer. Like a fool, he'd put off talking to her about their future because he didn't want to rock the boat, but now it might be too late. He might be sunk in a sea of his own procrastination.

Since Nicole had come home to Oak Hollow, he had tried to convince himself that she would end up staying, but he'd been a fool. She had made it clear from day one that her stay was only temporary.

But had he listened? Hell no.

He'd heard what he wanted, thinking that if he loved her enough that she'd want the same.

Fool.

He had climbed a damn tree to comfort her when she was so upset about not getting the other job that would have taken her away from him and Oak Hollow. Every time she'd checked her email or jumped at a phone call because she hoped it was about a job, it had been another small cut, adding up to a wound he now had to tend. Her determination and drive for the bistro and her writing and everything she did should have been a glaring clue that she wouldn't give up. And still he'd ignored all the signs.

She wasn't just going to suddenly change her career plans because he had fallen in love with her.

His beer was empty, so he made his way down to the bookstore and stood outside his closed office door, but there was only silence inside. Slowly, he opened the door and stepped inside to find Nicole sitting behind his desk with a piece of paper clutched in both hands. Her eyebrows were drawn together, and her shoulders were so tense they were up around her ears.

Light filtered through the white piece of paper, and he could make out a shadowy image of the other side. He had a bad feeling he knew what she was holding.

"What's that?" he asked.

She startled and the page dropped from her hands, fluttering onto the desktop. "Are *you* Ivy Moon?"

A flash chill made him shiver. He closed the office door behind him. "Where did you get that?"

"It was on the floor. I promise I wasn't snooping. Am I totally off base, or are you the author of my favorite book?"

He gave a quick nod and then pressed his fingertips to his forehead as if he could push out the last twelve hours. He'd already been in such a bad mood about her leaving him and now this.

"Liam, why didn't you tell me?"

"I don't tell anyone."

She gasped, and the look of hurt on her face was as powerful as a slap.

Nicole clasped her hands together, trying to stop the trembling. Was she just another "anyone" to him? She'd thought she was special, but it was an assumption she'd made before and look how that turned out. "You talked me into telling you all my darkest most personal and painful secrets. But you kept this from me."

"My family doesn't even know. Only me and a handful of other people do."

"Who?" She couldn't resist asking. She wanted to know who was more important than her.

"My editor, Rebecca. You met her at the conference. The publisher, someone in accounting and legal. And Sara Love is the one who talked me into writing the book. She runs the social media accounts for my pen name."

Every one of her muscles suddenly ached at once, and she didn't trust her legs to hold her upright if she stood. It made her unreasonably mad that Sara knew. "You had the perfect opportunity to tell me about your pen name after you met with Sara here in the bookstore. Right under my nose you two were talking about this big secret."

"I'm sorry. Truly."

"Liam, I told you things I never planned to tell anyone. Ever. And you wouldn't even trust me with this?"

"I can't risk it getting out."

"Why? Because you are a man writing romance?"

"No, it's more than that. I don't want a spotlight on me or to be asked to do interviews and appearances."

"The spotlight is exactly what most authors dream of."

"You know about the whole social media fiasco. If it gets out, that will all be dredged up from the depths." He ran a hand roughly through his hair and paced across the small space in front of his desk. "You know I hate being the center of attention."

"Which is why I won't give away your secret." When he remained silent, not meeting her eyes, she rubbed the heel of her palm against her chest where tension was gathering and restricting each breath. "But you didn't trust me to keep your secret."

He laced his fingers behind his head. "That's not it. It would have ruined the mystery and excitement if you had known."

His words bruised her. "Are you kidding me?"

That was a pitiful, hurtful excuse. He hadn't kept this from her to protect her excitement about a mystery author. There was more to it. Some other reason he didn't want her to know he had written her favorite book. "I am supposed to trust you with my deepest secrets, but you don't trust me with yours."

She could not be with another man who kept things from her.

When she came out from behind the desk, Liam stepped back as if to let her go past and out the door. Apparently, the conversation was over.

Her throat burned with the need to cry. And that was exactly what she would do once she was alone.

On legs that were still numb, she moved to the door, her palm sweaty and slick on the old metal doorknob.

"Nicole, sweetheart, wait. Please, don't go."

Liam held his breath as Nicole slowly turned to face him. There was hurt in her eyes that he had never meant to put there. He extended his hand, and every second she didn't take it felt like an eternity.

Ignoring his gesture, she stayed where she was.

"I'm so sorry, Nic." He let his arm drop to his side. "I've gotten so used to protecting this secret. I didn't think about how you would see it from your side."

"No, you didn't." She inhaled deeply and let it out even slower. "I do know what it's like to guard a secret. I did it for years and got really good at it. But I thought you and I had moved past keeping secrets from one another. Did you just like hearing me praise your book too much to tell me?" She pressed her fingertips hard against her mouth.

"No, Nic. That's not why." He'd waited too long to talk to her about this, but he'd been waiting to see if she was staying. It was selfish and stupid, and now…he wasn't even sure why he had thought he needed to keep this from her. "I can't deny I liked hearing the praise, but there is another reason I have put off telling you."

"Let's hear it." Her arms were clasped around her body as if she needed to hold herself together.

Now it was his turn to take a deep breath. "Why do you think you personally identify with the story so much?"

Her eyebrows drew together, and she thought for a moment and then her eyes widened. "Is the ex-boyfriend in the book supposed to be Jeff?"

"Yes. The idea for that character came to me after I overheard your conversation in the orchard that Thanksgiving. The story is about… You."

She backed up a few steps and bumped into the doorframe. "Oh, wow. I think… I think I need to be alone to process all of this. I'm taking the day off work tomorrow. There should be enough stock to get you through." She fumbled with the doorknob, finally got the door open and rushed away from him.

Liam stood perfectly still, letting his mistakes wash over him in a sea of salty regret. He didn't even know if she had gotten the job.

Chapter Twenty-Three

Nicole stood in the middle of her childhood bedroom, not sure what to do next. Her mom was out of
town for a couple of days with her boyfriend who'd
just come back to town, but that was fine with Nicole.
She wasn't ready to talk to her or Jenny or anyone else
about this mess. There was too much hurt and confu-
sion swirling inside her to even know where to begin.
Not to mention the problem of how she would talk
to her friends and family about what had happened
between them without giving away Liam's secret.

Even after this shocking revelation, she would
guard his secret like she had her own for so many
years.

Just when she'd been about to tell Liam that she
was in love with him and wanted to stay, the deci-

sion about whether or not to take the job had been made for her. She couldn't stay with another man who kept things from her. The choice was clear. Breaking her heart but clear.

She washed her face and then found her daughter in the living room. "Katie Cat, come sit down and let's talk."

"What's the matter, Mommy?"

"Nothing. I just want to tell you that I got a really great job offer." She was doing her very best to put on a happy face and be cheerful, but inside she was crumbling.

Her daughter looked at her warily and leaned away from her. "Where?"

"In Colorado. We have two different resorts to choose from."

Katie pressed her lips into a hard straight line, jumped up from the couch and ran upstairs. A few seconds later, a door slammed.

Nicole dropped her head into her hands and let the tears fall. She cried even harder in the shower, and then when she looked in on Katie, she was asleep, but there were tear tracks on both of her cheeks. It broke her heart to see her child upset, but she didn't want to wake her. There would be time to talk tomorrow, and she needed the night to figure out how to explain this to a child. There were too many things to sort out in her mind, and she didn't know where to begin.

She sat on her bed with her laptop, hoping that looking over the resort information would help her get excited about the job. But it didn't. It made her even sadder because the joy and thrill she should be feeling about this accomplishment was missing. She finally closed her laptop and climbed into bed.

In the stillness of the night, she replayed her conversation with Liam. When she'd told him that she knew what it was like to keep a secret, she'd meant it, and she was trying to see this situation from his point of view. Trying to figure out why he felt the need to keep it from her. Maybe he was embarrassed that the book was based on her life or thought she'd be upset about it? Because she really didn't want to believe that he thought she'd give away his secret.

Nicole rolled over in bed and punched her pillow into the right shape with a bit more force than necessary. She'd find the time to sit down with her mom and Jenny and get them to help her choose which resort would be best for them. Things at the bistro would have to be… Well, she wasn't sure what exactly to do about that, and she felt bad about it. She'd leave some recipes for things anyone could make and let Amy, Danny and Tina know they could call her. She and Katie would pack up her SUV, say their tearful goodbyes and start over. Again.

Monday morning, Liam needed two cups of strong coffee after a sleepless night. When he went downstairs, well before it was time to unlock the bookstore's front door, he looked up and stopped short. There was a crowd of people practically pressing their faces against the glass... And they had cameras.

"What the hell is going on?"

Cameras started to flash, and people were calling his name. And his pen name! His skin pricked into a field of goose bumps as if he'd been doused with a bucket of ice-cold betrayal. He let out a string of curse words he'd never say in front of other people.

My secret is out.

He spun away from the media circus outside his small-town bookstore and stalked behind one of the bookshelves. With his back pressed against the rows of self-help volumes, he took a few slow breaths, but it wasn't helping. He had worked hard to create a comfortable life here in his little hometown. A place he could quietly live his life while staying out of the media and the public eye.

"How? Why is this happening?" His gut roiled, and his head pounded with thoughts that he did not want to believe were even a possibility. But the evidence...

His pen name had remained a secret for over a year, and the morning after Nicole found out the truth, the press was knocking at his door. It wasn't like her to do anything to hurt someone. Was she that mad at him that she'd told someone by accident?

On purpose? Surely not. Was it to let it be known she was writing with a famous author in hopes of getting published?

Was this why Nicole took the day off?

However it had happened, his secret was out, and there was no reason to put it off. Getting it over with would be better than dragging it out. He took another moment to gather himself and then walked to the front doors and let the reporters inside. There weren't as many as he'd first thought, but it was very likely that more would show up at some point.

They were all talking at once. He stood there with his arms crossed over his chest and didn't say a word. After a minute, they got the message that he wasn't going to answer questions until there was some order to this chaos. He eventually took questions and explained his reasons for why he had wanted it to stay a secret, without bringing up the social media fiasco. No need for him to be the one who reopened that can of garbage. He asked them to respect his privacy, but he would have to wait and see how that request turned out.

As they were all leaving, he asked how they'd found out he was the author, and one of them handed him a copy of the *Oak Hollow Herald*. It was folded open to the column written by Mrs. Jenkins.

You heard it here first, folks! We have a celebrity hidden in our midst. Our very own Liam Mendez, owner of Sip & Read bookstore, is

*also a bestselling author. You won't find his
name on a book cover because he has been
using a secret pen name. A pen name many
of you have heard. He is none other than Ivy
Moon.*

He stopped reading, locked the front door without opening the bookstore and stomped up the stairs
to his apartment, reminding himself of his teenager. At least he knew where to go to discover the
source of the leak. But before he called Mrs. Jenkins, he needed to call Sara so they could plan what
to say on the social media accounts she managed
for him. He dialed her number, and she picked up
on the first ring.

"How mad are you? Do you totally hate me?"
Sara asked.

He braced a hand on his kitchen counter. "Hate
you? Why?"

"Because… Don't you know yet?"

He gasped. "It was you? You told Mrs. Jenkins?"

"Well, yes."

"What the hell, Sara?" He was trying not to yell,
but it was hard.

"I'm sorry. Please, let me explain how it all happened."

He dropped onto the couch and leaned forward
with his forehead pressed against the palm of his
hand. "Start talking."

She explained how she'd had four glasses of wine

before her interview with Mrs. Jenkins. She'd been asked about Ivy Moon, and one thing led to another. Sara had made a spur of the moment decision that they could use the publicity to promote the next book that she had just helped him plot.

"I can't believe you did this."

"I messed up, Liam. What if I announce that I am the author known as Ivy Moon, and I was just trying to throw them off the trail?"

"It's too late. I already had reporters show up at the bookstore, and I admitted it."

She uttered a cuss word he'd never heard her say. "I shouldn't drink that much wine and be allowed to talk to people."

"Clearly."

"At the time, I thought the truth of your pen name coming out would end up being a good thing, but I made a mistake and I hope you will eventually forgive me."

"I'm sure it will all work out." He really hoped that statement was true. "I need to go and tend to some business."

"I'll make this up to you, somehow."

"We'll talk later."

Liam ended the call and dropped his phone onto the cushion beside him. He would have to seriously consider if he could continue working with Sara, but there was one bright spot to their phone call.

It had not been Nicole who told his secret.

* * *

When Nicole woke the next morning, Katie was standing beside her bed and the sun was higher in the sky than it usually was when she woke up.

"Come cuddle with me, sweetie." She lifted the covers and her daughter climbed in beside her, and for a few moments they were silent.

"Mommy, do you love Liam?"

Such a simple question, with so many complications. "Yes, I do love him."

"So do I. Why do we have to leave? You already have a good job."

Her child wasn't wrong about that. It might not come with the perks of the resort, but she loved working at the bistro. "You don't want to move to a new exciting place?"

"No. Here we have Mimi, Aunt Jenny and Uncle Eric, and Lilly, and Liam, and Travis. I have new friends at school and my friend Hannah. I love the bookstore and I love Oak Hollow."

"You are a smart girl, Katie Cat." She kissed the top of her head. "I tell you what. Let me do a bit of thinking and then I need to talk to Liam."

Katie sighed and relaxed in her arms but then sat up. "I'm going downstairs to eat a bowl of cereal so you can get started on your thinking." She hopped out of the bed but then paused at the door and looked over her shoulder. "While you're thinking, remember all the good things I said about living here."

Nicole smiled but was fighting tears. "I promise I will think about everyone and everything you said."

"Good. I love you."

"I love you, too, Katie Cat."

After staring at the ceiling for a few more minutes and getting nothing resolved, Nicole got up, dressed in jeans and a sweatshirt and then went downstairs. "Katie, I'm going to go take a walk in the orchard. Just come outside and ring the bell on the porch if you need me."

"Okay. That's a good place to think. I'll be fine." Katie got up from the kitchen table to hug her before Nicole went outside.

The spidery winter branches of the youngest peach trees swayed in the cold breeze, looking forlorn as they scratched against the cloudy gray sky. Waiting for the sun and spring rain to help them blossom with new growth. For years, she'd been sure of what she wanted, but everything had been turned topsy-turvy.

She had been so angry at Jeff for so long. Blaming him for so many problems in her life. But she'd been at fault, too. She had been complacent and stayed with him too long, allowing him to make her feel bad about spending money on school and having dreams. He had played on her need for perfection and success and made it worse, making her think she had to reach a certain place, or she would be a failure and he'd get to say he'd told her so.

Nicole sat down under one of the old pecan trees

and leaned her back against the sturdy trunk. She'd let her husband—the man who was supposed to be her partner and biggest supporter—rule the way she thought about herself. It no longer mattered what he said or thought about her dreams or goals. She would no longer let him have that power over her.

Looking up at the morning sky, some things about her life were becoming clear.

I hope you rest in peace, Jeff. But I'm done letting you get in my head.

Nicole got up and headed for the house with a plan forming in her mind. She knew what she had to do. Liam had said his story was about her. If the ex in the story was based on Jeff, she was the heroine. The one who had gotten herself out of a bad situation, started over, found love and made something of herself. Like the heroine in *Her New Life*, she was ready to make a change not only to where they lived but in the way she thought about herself.

Being successful wasn't only about prestige or money. It was happiness and love. As for setting a better example, a happy mom living an authentic life seemed like a good place to start.

Now, she needed to talk to Liam. She hadn't told him she loved him, and he hadn't said it either. But she had felt his love in so many ways that she had little doubt. This issue with the secret pen name was something they could talk about and get past. She of all people understood secrets and the way you could be twisted into thinking you needed to keep them.

After Liam sent the reporters away, he'd only intended to delay opening the bookstore, but after a few minutes he texted his employees and told them they had the day off with pay. Instead of running his business, he stayed upstairs where he sat on his couch in the dark. No TV. No music. Just the sound of his own breathing and his aching heartbeat. It wasn't Nicole who told his secret, but she was still leaving Oak Hollow. And him. He loved her with all of his heart, but that did not give him the right to ask her to give up her dream. He just wished there was a woman who would put him first.

Travis walked in the door from school and flipped on the light and then startled. "What are you doing sitting here in the dark?"

"Nothing." *Nothing but feeling sorry for myself.* He was losing the woman he loved.

"Why is the bookstore closed?"

"Sit down, son. We have a few things to talk about."

Travis dropped his backpack on the floor. "Should I be scared?"

"No. There is nothing for you to worry about." He told him about writing the book under a secret pen name and the media showing up. He admitted to keeping the secret from Nicole and about her getting a job she'd hoped for.

His son crossed his arms over his chest and shook his head. "Dad, you are being stupid."

"Excuse me?" His slouched shoulders straightened and stiffened. He did not need his son talking to him like that on top of his heart breaking.

"You're going to blow this whole thing with Nicole. I understand why you didn't fight to keep Mom, but why are you doing it now?"

The comment cut like the jagged teeth of a serrated knife. His thoughts flashed to the day when his wife told him that she was leaving him for someone else. Someone who understood her and her job commitments. With Nicole it wasn't another man, but there was still something drawing her away from him. Was he feeling sorry for himself? Hell yes. But what else could he do?

He met his son's eyes. "Nic wants a big career in the culinary world. Who am I to try and take that away from her?"

Travis flopped back on the couch with a sound of frustration only a teenager could produce. "You have always told me to work hard for what I want and to fight for my dreams."

"That's true." He had said that over and over because he desperately wanted his child to have a happy fulfilled life.

"Dad…" His son's voice broke off, and then he sat up and he shook his head of dark brown hair that flopped over his forehead. "Lots of the time, you put other people's feelings ahead of yours. But it was nice to see you happy with her. We were doing things like a family, and it was good. You also said that on top of working hard, sometimes all you need to do is just ask for what you want. Did you even talk to Nicole about staying here?"

"No." He'd kept putting it off waiting for the time to be right.

"Where is this job she got?" Travis asked.

"I don't know." Nicole hadn't said. She also had never said that she'd gotten the job. He just assumed she did. What if she had *not* and that's why she'd was so upset?

"Shouldn't you find out?"

His son was right. He deserved a happily-ever-after ending too. "How did you get so wise?"

"Unless you do something about this, I won't be able to say I got my smarts from you."

"Do you have any brilliant advice for how your old dad should do that?"

"As you just admitted to me, you are a writer. Apparently, a famous one. Use your words," his son said on his way to his bedroom.

With the lights on, Liam could see his distorted reflection on the surface of the television screen, and he did not like what he saw. He had kept things from the woman he loved because he was... Like his son had said, stupid. Nicole had been right to be upset with him. He'd encouraged her to spill her painful secrets, but he had kept quiet, some-how believing and rationalizing that it was okay for him to do it.

Hopefully Nicole had had enough time alone to think because she needed to hear what he had to say. He loved her with all of his heart and even if it was across a distance, he wanted to mend their re-lationship and keep her in his life in whatever way she would have him.

If he could write a book that Nicole loved, he could use his "words" to mend what he had broken. The best place he could think of to start was with the simplest of words. Words that carried a lot of power. *I'm sorry and I love you.*

He got up off the couch and stretched to ease the stiffness from sitting for so long in one posi-tion. Grabbing his cell phone, he typed out a text message.

Can I see you? I really want to talk.

Her reply came fast. Meet you on the rooftop in two hours.

Relief that Liam wanted to talk was flooding through Nicole's body and mind. She had been plan-ning to go to him, but knowing he wanted her to, made her fill with hope that they could make their relationship work.

She thought about her nine-year-old's reaction to

her announcement that she'd gotten a job in another state, far away from the place and the people where they'd found happiness and support. And love. She had never been happier in a job than she was at Sip & Read. A small-town bistro in the back of a bookstore run by the man of her dreams. There was no huge kitchen full of professional staff, only young people eager to learn, but there was no place else she would rather be. No other man she wanted to work with. Nicole knew what she wanted for the rest of her life. Now, she just had to go and get it.

One of the classes she'd attended at the writers' convention had talked about making a grand gesture, and what better way for her to do that than to combine baking with writing. In her mother's kitchen, she baked a large sugar cookie that she freehand cut to look like an open book. It was cooling while she mixed icing in several colors.

Katie skipped around the kitchen table. "Are you going to tell him you love him, Mommy?"

"Yes, I am. I'm planning to write a message on this big cookie. Any idea what I should say?"

Her daughter stopped beside her at the counter and propped her chin on both hands. "You can make it look like a fancy card. You could ask him to marry you."

She laughed at her child's enthusiasm. "That might be too much too soon."

"I guess so. Maybe he will ask you."

She kissed the top of her head. "You really want to plan a wedding, don't you?"

"Of course. I like weddings. If you and Liam have one, I can be a flower girl."

Nicole chuckled again. It took her about half an hour to decorate it with details and her message written across the two pages. She put it in a flat shirt box. Katie went over to stay with Abuela, and Nicole headed to Sip & Read.

When she climbed the stairs to the rooftop, Liam was already there, standing at one side looking out over the square.

He turned at her approach, and his smile was both tender and nervous. "Hi, sweetheart. I'm glad you came."

"I'm glad you wanted me to."

He took a few steps toward her. "Can I talk first?"

"Sure."

"I made a mistake."

Her throat tightened and made her breath stutter. What if he wasn't going to say what she hoped, and he was ending things? She put the box with the cookie on the table before she dropped it.

"Travis said since I'm a writer I should use my words, and there are so many of them to choose from in infinite combinations, but I'll start with the most important. "I love you, Nic."

Her relief was quick, but before she could respond, he continued.

"I should have told you sooner." He closed the rest of the distance between them. "I love you with all of my heart, and I am so sorry about keeping my pen name a secret from you. Travis, in his teenage wisdom, told me I was being stupid, and he isn't wrong."

She chuckled and opened her arms, so relieved when he encircled her waist and pulled her close. "I love you, too. So much."

He kissed her and then put his forehead against hers. "I have to know. Where is your new job?"

Her smile grew. He thought she was leaving. That's why he was so upset. "Well, I'm hoping it's downstairs, if you'll have me?"

He cradled one of her cheeks. "Sweetheart, of course I'll have you. Nothing would make me happier."

"When I was offered the job with Hamilton Resorts, I was given a choice of two locations, but that was my old dream."

"Are you sure? You need to be completely certain that you won't have regrets."

"More than sure. There is nowhere else I would rather be than right here with you. I made you something." She nodded to the box and eased from his embrace to lift the lid. "I had all these big ideas about what to write, but it came down to this."

Love takes time. It's a thousand tiny moments layered one atop of the other, and I want to keep building that with you. You are the love of my life.

He grinned. "I love that message. We have so much history together and it's perfect."

"I want to take the first steps of my new life with you. You have fulfilled several of my wishes. The crush I had for so many years is now a relationship. I know the identity of my favorite author, *and* I get to work with him."

He chuckled and kissed her. "Yes, you do. Think of the scenes we can act out and write."

"Oh, I have. But there is something else. You have helped me discover what real success truly is. You have shown me what it is to truly love and be loved by a man."

"And I want to keep showing you every single day of your life." He held her close once again and breathed in against her hair. "Katie asked me what a prologue was. And for us, I think that was our childhood. I can't wait to write our story together, from the first page to the last."

Her cheeks were starting to ache from smiling. "I'm ready and excited to write that story with you."

He dropped to one knee and took both of her hands in his. "Nicole, will you be the epilogue of my life?"

"Yes, Liam. I absolutely will. I'll be right here beside you for every word."

He pulled off his college ring and slipped it onto her left hand. "Now, you are my girl for life."

"I love the sound of that.'

He stood and lifted her off her feet, kissing her with a passion big enough to start making up for all the lost years. "You know, I think this is going to be a bestseller."

"I believe you are right. What should our first chapter be?"

He took her hand and laced their fingers. "Kiss me again, and then let's go tell the kids that we are going to be a real family."

Epilogue

Liam's pen name being revealed to the world had not been the nightmare that he'd once thought it would. A few more reporters had shown up and he got calls about interviews and he did a few when he knew the person had a good reputation. Business at the bookstore and around the whole town square had increased, and that was good for his community.

But he'd groaned in protest when Nicole cut out a quote from one article and taped it onto the back of their bedroom door.

The creative mind behind Ivy Moon's bestselling romance novel is not in the body of a woman as you'd expect but instead in a man who looks like he should be gracing the cover rather than writing the words on the pages.

She said it reminded her of how lucky she was to have his mind *and* body in her life.

Nicole's Bistro had become popular in its own right, and she was also asked for interviews and made the cover of one magazine. Travis and Nicole continued to make cooking videos that were rapidly gaining in popularity, and his son had asked to live permanently with them in Oak Hollow.

Thankfully, none of the old negativity had resurfaced on social media, and Sara Love no longer handled the accounts for Ivy Moon. His lovely bride-to-be had taken over that task and the theme of his accounts—now using his real name beside his alias—had shifted from all books to include a small glimpse of the family life behind the author. The family who needed a bit more space than their current apartment provided.

Liam pulled back the thick sheet of plastic hanging across the opening they'd cut in the living room wall. Nicole's brother-in-law, Eric McKnight, had made good progress on the construction today. The unused attic space had been framed and was taking the shape of a family room, master bedroom and bath and an office for Nicole that looked out over the town square. Having two girls in the house had also shown him the need for a second bathroom.

"Liam," Nicole yelled as her rapid footsteps pounded on the stairs. "Babe, where are you?"

He pushed the plastic aside and stepped back

into the living room, loving that she'd started calling him by that term of endearment. "I'm right here. What has put that big grin on your face? Did we win the lottery?"

"In a way, I did." Her green eyes were sparkling. "I just got an offer to publish my book!"

"That's amazing, honey." He hugged her tight enough to lift her off her feet. "I never had any doubt that you would. You are a multi-talented woman."

With her arms still wrapped around his neck, she smiled up at him. "Which one is your favorite talent?"

"The one only I know about," he whispered against her ear, making her shiver and giggle.

"I'm going to miss you tonight. What are you and the guys going to do for your last night as a single guy?"

"Anson, Eric and the whole gang are coming over here. We are just going to hang out and play cards. What kind of wild night do you ladies have planned over at Mimi's house?"

"Drinking champagne and laughing while we pamper ourselves with beauty treatments."

"Want a bit of pampering right now?" Liam nuzzled his face against her neck.

She sighed and kissed him once more before stepping back. "I'd love nothing more, but that might have to wait. The kids will be home—"

The door opened halfway. "We're home." Travis called out then opened it the rest of the way and eyed them. "I've learned to give a warning, so I don't catch y'all kissing like teenagers."

Liam and Nicole tried not to laugh, but they did.

"Hi, Mommy." Katie came in behind Travis and hugged Nicole around her waist and then paused in front of Liam with her hands on her hips and her head tilted. "Since the wedding is tomorrow, do you think maybe I can start calling you... Dad?"

Liam opened his arms and pulled the little girl in for a hug, taking a few heartbeats to make sure his voice wouldn't break with emotion before he spoke. "I would love that. I've always wanted a daughter, and I couldn't ask for a better one than you, Katie Cat."

Nicole wiped a tear from the corner of her eye and smiled at him in a way that made him feel like the luckiest man in the world.

On a beautiful spring day, Nicole stood in front of the full-length mirror in her mom's bedroom. Her heart was full to overflowing with happiness and love as she stood with her mother, sister and daughter admiring the wedding dress Jenny had designed just for her. It was an ivory vintage-style gown with lace applique on the bodice, on the flowy butterfly sleeves and sprinkled about on the skirt. It had a V-neck and an even deeper V in the back with a row of tiny buttons down to her waist, and she'd never felt more beautiful.

"Mommy, you look so amazing," Katie said from beside her. "Can I wear that dress someday?"

"Thank you, sweetie. Of course you can wear it." She took her daughter's hands and held her arms out. "Look at how beautiful you are." Her pale pink dress was made from the same silky fabric as Mimi and Jenny's dresses, but they were each a different style befitting their age.

"Are you ready for your crown of peach blossoms?" Jenny asked. Their artist friend, Alexandra, had arrived that morning to create a floral crown of fresh pink blossoms and baby's breath.

"Yes. I think that is the final touch and then I'll be ready to walk down the aisle."

There was a knock at the door. "Is everyone dressed," Travis said from the other side.

"Yes, come in," Nicole called out.

Jenny opened the door for Travis, and he held up his new camera. "Wow. You all look really pretty. Want me to take a few photos?"

"Yes, please. It's perfect timing," Mimi said. "You can get some shots of me putting on her crown of flowers."

He took candid shots and then they moved into the living room and stood in front of the fireplace. "Now stand in order of age," the teenager said. "I printed a whole list of wedding photos to take, and one was to line up the family generations."

Nicole was so touched that her talented stepson had taken the time and was so invested in the wedding. With her mother on her right and then Jenny and Katie on her left, they all smiled for the camera.

The orchard was in full bloom. A sea of pink blossoms shimmered in the sunshine and perfumed the air with sweetness that reminded her of her childhood. Travis ran ahead of them so he could take his spot next to his father and the other groomsmen. The professional photographer would get shots of them coming down the aisle that they had created between two rows of the biggest peach trees that were closest to the river. The subtle sound of rushing water mingled with birdsongs as they neared the white wooden folding screen that had been put up to block them from view until the moment the ceremony started.

Mimi looked around the screen and gave the musicians, Alexandra Walker and her father, a thumbs up. Soft music from two guitars made Nicole's heart flutter like a hummingbird's. This was the moment she'd been waiting for. She was about to marry the man of her dreams.

"Mom, thank you for making everything so beautiful and special today," Nicole said.

"I love you, sweetheart. I'm so proud of you." Mimi kissed her cheek and then made her way to her seat on the front row of white chairs that they'd set up in the open space where the peach and pecan orchards met.

"I am so happy for you," Jenny said, and then started down the aisle to the flower-covered arbor where Liam would be waiting.

Nicole held out her hand to her daughter. "Are you ready to walk me down the aisle?"

"I'm ready." Katie took her hand, and with the other she lifted her small bouquet of peach blossoms to her nose.

When they stepped into view, her eyes locked with Liam's across the distance and her whole body tingled. Standing beneath an arbor covered with fresh flowers, he put a hand over his heart and smiled in a way she knew meant his emotions were close to the surface. Another shimmer of love washed over her like sunshine and a soft breeze.

In the place where she'd taken her first steps to a five-year-old Liam so many years ago, she returned his beaming smile and put one foot in front of the other, taking the steps that would join their lives forever.

* * * * *

#2959 FORTUNE'S DREAM HOUSE
The Fortunes of Texas: Hitting the Jackpot • by Nina Crespo

For Max Fortune Maloney to get his ranch bid accepted, he has to convince his agent, Eliza Henry, to pretend they're heading for the altar. Eliza needs the deal to advance her career, but she fears jeopardizing her reputation almost as much as she does falling for the sweet-talking cowboy.

#2960 SELLING SANDCASTLE
The McFaddens of Tinsley Cove • by Nancy Robards Thompson

Moving to North Carolina to be a part of a reality real estate show was never in newly divorced Cassie Houston's plans but she needs a fresh start. That fresh start was not going to include romance—still, the sparks flying between her and fellow costar Logan McFadden are impossible to deny. But they both have difficult pasts and sparks might not be enough.

#2961 THE COWBOY'S MISTAKEN IDENTITY
Dawson Family Ranch • by Melissa Senate

While looking for his father, rancher Chase Dawson finds an irate woman. *How could he abandon her and their son?* The problem is, Chase doesn't have a baby. But he does have a twin. Chase vows to right his brother's wrongs and be the man Hannah Calhoun and his nephew need. Can his love break through Hannah's guarded heart?

#2962 THE VALENTINE'S DO-OVER
by Michelle Lindo-Rice

When radio personalities Selena Cartwright and Trent Moon share why they've sworn off love and hate Valentine's Day, the gala celebrating singlehood is born! Planning the event has Trent and Selena seeing, and wanting, each other more than just professionally. As the gala approaches, can they overcome past heartache and possibly discover that Trent + Selena = True Love 4-Ever?

#2963 VALENTINES FOR THE RANCHER
Aspen Creek Bachelors • by Kathy Douglass

Jillian Adams expected Miles Montgomery to propose—she got a breakup speech instead! Now Jillian is back, and their ski resort hometown is heating up! Their kids become inseparable, making it impossible to avoid each other. So when the rancher asks Jillian for forgiveness and a Valentine's Day dance, can she trust him, and her heart, this time?

#2964 WHAT HAPPENS IN THE AIR
Love in the Valley • by Michele Dunaway

After Luke Thornton shattered her heart, Shelby Bien fled town to become a jet-setting photographer. Shelby's shocked to find that single dad Luke's back in New Charles. When they join forces to fly their families' hot-air balloon, it's Shelby's chance at a cover story. And, just maybe, a second chance for the former sweethearts' own story!

HARLEQUIN
PLUS

Try the best multimedia subscription service for romance readers like you!

Read, Watch and Play.

Experience the easiest way to get the romance content you crave.

Start your **FREE TRIAL** at
<u>www.harlequinplus.com/freetrial</u>.